Oliver Optic

Little by Little

Or, The Cruise of the Flyaway; a Story for Young Folks

Oliver Optic

Little by Little
Or, The Cruise of the Flyaway; a Story for Young Folks

ISBN/EAN: 9783744769600

Printed in Europe, USA, Canada, Australia, Japan

Cover: Foto ©Andreas Hilbeck / pixelio.de

More available books at **www.hansebooks.com**

LITTLE BY LITTLE.
OR THE
CRUISE OF THE
FLYAWAY.

BY
OLIVER
OPTIC.

CINCINNATI,
RICKEY, MALLORY & CO.

LITTLE BY LITTLE;

OR,

THE CRUISE OF THE FLYAWAY.

A Story for Young Folks.

BY

OLIVER OPTIC,

AUTHOR OF "THE BOAT CLUB," "ALL ABOARD," "NOW OR NEVER,"
"TRY AGAIN," "POOR AND PROUD," "IN DOORS AND OUT,"
ETC. ETC.

CINCINNATI:

RICKEY, MALLORY & CO.

BOSTON: CROSBY, NICHOLS, LEE & CO.

NEW YORK: PHINNEY, BLAKEMAN & MASON.

1861.

PREFACE.

IN presenting to his young friends the sixth volume of the "Library for Young People," the author cannot be unconscious of what the readers of his former books require of him. They will turn the leaves of "Little by Little," expecting to find an abundance of stirring incidents; and he hopes they will not be disappointed. Some of the older readers and sterner critics will look for romantic and rather exaggerated events; but he thinks they will look in vain, for as we grow older we become more reasonable, and do not expect showers of gold to fall upon every seedy hero, or to see nice young gentlemen leap over lofty precipices without sometimes being dashed to pieces.

But the author hopes that something more than exciting incidents will be found upon his pages; that, though he has seldom, if ever, gone out of his way to define the moral quality, or measure the moral quantity, of the words and deeds of his characters, the story will not be found wanting in a true Christian spirit.

1 *

Paul Duncan, the hero of this volume, is a nautical young gentleman, and most of the events of the story occur upon the water; but the author hopes his young lady friends will not make faces at him on this account. The boys insisted upon having a sea story, and being the "lords of creation," of course they must be indulged; but the writer most solemnly promises to remember the girls next time.

Thanking my young friends again for the continued kindness manifested towards my pets, I give them "Little by Little," hoping that the excellent spirit of Paul Duncan will pervade their minds and hearts, and lead them forward to the material and moral triumphs which crowned his useful life.

WILLIAM T. ADAMS.

DORCHESTER, August 28, 1860.

CONTENTS.

		PAGE
CHAP. I.— Paul Duncan disobeys Orders. .		11
CHAP. II.— Paul is cool and self-possessed.		25
CHAP. III.— Paul hears bad News.		38
CHAP. IV.— Paul becomes the Head of the Family.		52
CHAP. V.— Paul cooks his own Breakfast, and goes a-fishing.		66
CHAP. VI.— Paul makes a good Speculation.		79
CHAP. VII.— Paul goes into Business on his own Account.		93
CHAP VIII. — Paul takes a Cold Bath.		107
CHAP. IX.— Paul becomes Skipper of the Fawn.		120
CHAP. X.— Paul and John are very much excited. .		134
CHAP. XI.— Paul's First Cruise in the Fawn. .		147
CHAP. XII.— Paul sleeps on his Watch.		160
CHAP. XIII.— Paul makes a Night Run in the Storm. .		173
CHAP. XIV.— Paul scolds the First Officer of the Fawn.		186
CHAP. XV.— Paul goes on a Cruise in the Flyaway.		198
CHAP. XVI. — Paul witnesses a Mutiny.		211

(7)

8 CONTENTS.

PAGE

CHAP. XVII. — Paul discovers that Mischief is brewing. . 224

CHAP. XVIII. — Paul is made a Prisoner.. 237

CHAP. XIX. — Paul takes Command of the Flyaway. . . 250

CHAP. XX. — Paul exercises a strong moral Influence. . . 263

CHAP. XXI. — Paul advances Little by Little, and the Story
ends. 275

LITTLE BY LITTLE.

LITTLE BY LITTLE;

OR,

THE CRUISE OF THE FLYAWAY.

CHAPTER I.

PAUL DUNCAN DISOBEYS ORDERS.

"I'LL give you a quarter, Paul, if you will take me down to the Point in your boat," said Thomas Nettle, as he came down to the beach where the boy addressed was baling out an old dingy-looking boat.

"It blows too hard," replied Paul Duncan.

"The club went down in their boat."

"But it didn't blow so hard then as it does now. It's a regular sou'easter."

"What are you afraid of, Paul?"

"I'm not afraid; but there's no use of risking your life for a quarter."

"I'll give you a half, then."

Paul Duncan hesitated. Half a dollar was a great deal of money to him, and more than often found its way into his exchequer. He glanced at the white-capped waves in the bay, and then at Thomas.

"There's no ballast in her," said he.

"Put some rocks in, then."

"I think it's rather dangerous, and I don't believe your mother would agree to have you go out in a boat in such a blow as this."

"My mother! Humph! Let me tell you I'm not tied to my mother's apron string. I think I'm old enough to have a will of my own. Don't talk to me about my mother," replied Thomas, contemptuously. "I'm not a baby."

"Just as you please; but I think it blows too hard to go out."

"Let me have your boat, and I'll go alone then, if you are afraid to go."

"I'm not afraid," answered Paul, stung by these repeated implications upon his courage. "Jump in, and I'll give you enough of it before you get half way to the Point."

Thomas got into the boat, which was any thing but a beauty in her shape and appointments. Paul pushed her off the beach upon which she had grounded, and as she receded from the shore, leaped on board of her. Placing an oar at the stern, he sculled her out a short distance from the land, and then shook out the sail. The first flaw of wind that struck it heeled the boat over so far that Thomas leaped with desperate haste up to the windward side.   .   .

"Don't be afraid, Tom," said Paul, with a smile. "She has got the wind now."

"Who's afraid?" demanded Thomas.

"I thought you were by the way you jumped."

"Well, the gunnel of your old craft went under."

"Not quite."

"I say it did; and you don't suppose I was

2

going to sit there and be spilled into the drink—
do you?" continued Thomas, sharply.

"I won't dispute with you; she heeled over,
as a boat always will when she first gets the wind."

"You think you are an old salt, Paul, but you
don't know enough to navigate a herring pond."

"Just as you like," replied Paul, whose good
nature was proof against the assaults of his companion. "I don't pretend to know much; but I
think I understand this old boat pretty well."

"Paul! Paul!" cried a voice from the shore.

"That's my mother," said the young boatman,
as he discovered a woman on the beach. "What
do you want, mother?"

"Come ashore," replied Mrs. Duncan, whose
voice was almost drowned by the noise of the
waves as they beat against the boat.

Paul's mother seemed to think she had said
enough, for her son was generally a very obedient
boy, and she turned to walk up the bluff towards
the house. But she knew enough about the management of a boat to perceive that, in this instance,
her order was not obeyed.

"Come ashore right off, Paul," she repeated with an emphasis that was calculated to make an impression upon the rebellious party.

"Do you want me, mother?" asked Paul, as he put the boat about, and brought her upon the home tack.

"No, I don't want you; but it blows too hard for you to be out there. You'll capsize, as true as you're alive," replied Mrs. Duncan; and seeing the boat headed towards the shore, she hastened home.

"Are you going to back out, Paul?" demanded Thomas, as the boat came about.

"My mother won't let me go," replied Paul, rather sheepishly, for he was not proof against the derision of his companion.

"Won't let you go!" sneered Thomas.

"You heard what she said."

"I did; my mother would no more dare to say as much as that to me than she would dare to cut my head off. She knows her place better."

Paul was not a little shocked by this unfeeling speech, and could not help seeing that Thomas had not much regard for his mother. For his own part, he loved his mother very much, though he was not exactly willing to confess the fact to a boy who entertained such opinions as those of Thomas Nettle. He had been accustomed to obey his mother for the respect and love he bore her, and it had never before occurred to him that she overstepped the bounds of reason and propriety in presuming to command him. Paul had the reputation of being a good boy, both at home and among the neighbors; but it must not be inferred that he was perfect, that he never disobeyed his father and mother,—though the instances were very rare,—or that he never did what he knew to be wrong. He had his faults and his weaknesses; but for the present I shall let my young reader discover them from what he says and what he does. He was disturbed by the derision of his friend, no less than by his impudent self-possession. He even asked himself why he should be tied to his mother's apron string, as Thomas expressed the subjection of the child to the parent. He was only a year younger than his companion, and he began to question whether it was not about time for him to assert his own independence, and cut the apron string when it pulled too hard upon his inclination.

Paul was the oldest of a family of six children, and was now in his fourteenth year. His father was a journeyman ship carpenter — an honest, temperate, hard-working man, who was obliged to struggle with the realities of life in order to win a comfortable subsistence for his large family. In the inoffensive sense of the term, he was a poor man; that is, he lived from hand to mouth, and had not saved a single dollar with which to meet the misfortunes of life. But he had brought up his family as well as he could, and given the oldest the best education his limited means would afford.

Thomas Nettle's father was a wealthy merchant, who had retired from active business, and lived upon his beautiful estate in Bayville, in which transpired the events of my story. Major Nettle,

2*

as his townsmen called him, — for he had attained
to the rank indicated by his military title in the
militia, — was an easy, careless man, and had but a
very low appreciation of the moral and religious duties and responsibilities of a parent. It was a favorite theory with him that a boy would do well enough
if only let alone. It was of no use to cram his
head or his heart with notions, as he called them,
about morality and religion; the boy would find
them out himself when he wanted them. In support of his doctrine, he used to point to the minister's son who was in the state prison, and the
deacon's son who had run away to sea to avoid
the house of correction. Of course, then, Master
Thomas Nettle's parental training was never very
severe, for he had no one to dispute his independence when he chose to assert it.

Paul had seen enough of the world to find out
that wealth commands a certain respect, and he
could not always keep down a sense of deference
with which his rich companions inspired him; and
when they admitted him to their friendship, he

could not help being greatly influenced by their words and their actions. Thomas was always dressed well, and always had money in his pocket; and these things made Paul realize the difference in their social positions. It is true, he tried to make himself believe that he was as good as any one else, and would not bend his neck or his knee to the smartest boy in Bayville; yet he could not but feel the disparity between himself and the sons of his rich neighbors. He would not go out of his way to court their favor, though it flattered his vanity to be their chosen companion.

"Steady! why don't you luff her up, when the puffs come," said Thomas, as a flaw of wind struck the sail, and careened her so far that she took in a little water over the side.

"O, I don't mind a little dash of water over the side," replied Paul, with a smile; for it must be owned that he was disposed to punish his companion for the imputations he had cast upon his seamanship and his courage.

"Well, are you going ashore?" continued

Thomas. "Are you going to let your mother domineer over you? If you do, I hope she will put you in the cradle and rock you to sleep when you get ashore."

"We must get some ballast," answered Paul, who had not yet got far enough to declare his independence of maternal authority.

"You are afraid to go!"

"I think I can stand it as long as you can."

"Then what are you going ashore for?"

"After more ballast," replied Paul, who, though deeply stung by the sneers of Thomas, had not yet decided to disobey his mother.

"Will you take me down to the Point when you get the ballast?"

"I don't know; I'll see."

The old boat dashed on, and in a moment or two grounded upon the beach. There was a great struggle in the soul of Paul. He did not like to go contrary to the express command of his mother on the one hand, and he did not like to incur the derision of Thomas on the other, for he would tell it to all the boys, who would call him " chickenish."

" There are two rocks that will just answer your purpose," said Thomas, as they leaped out of the boat. " You take one and I will take the other. Come, bear a hand, or I shall not get to the picnic till the fun is all over."

The two large stones were placed in the boat, and still Paul was undecided. He had not the courage to face the ridicule of his independent friend, nor the heart to disobey the mother whom he loved and respected.

" I guess I won't go, Tom," said he, as a momentary resolution supported the better impulse of his nature.

" Chicken-hearted ! Are you afraid of your mother or of the wind and waves ? " sneered Thomas, and his features curled up into an expression of contempt which moved the hesitating boy quite as much as his words.

" Of neither. If you think I'm afraid to go any where that you dare go, you are very much mistaken. It's a very easy thing for you to stand there and talk, but when the boat takes in a pint of water over the side, you jump as though an earthquake had taken you all aback," said Paul, smartly.

" Humph ! Get into the boat, and we'll soon see who's afraid ; though perhaps you had better go and get your mother to go with you."

" I have proved you to be a coward, and I don't think there is any use of going now. I don't like to be in a boat with a fellow who is skittish when the wind blows," continued Paul, who was determined to make the most of their previous experience. " It isn't safe to have a fellow jumping about in the boat when there's a heavy sea on. You might upset her, cantering about over the thwarts like a frightened colt."

" You are smart, Paul ; but your big talk sounds silly while I stand here and stump you to carry me down to the Point. You are afraid of the sea, and afraid of your mother. You dare not go !"

" Jump in !" cried Paul, desperately. as his failing resolution fled before these taunts. "Jump in, Tom."

"Now don't back out if you happen to see one of your mother's aprons on the clothes-line."

"Never fear me; and if you don't wish yourself ashore before you get half way to Tenean Point, I lose my guess; that's all," answered Paul, as he pushed the boat off into deep water. "The wind is dead ahead, and we must beat all the way down."

"Put her through, Paul."

"Ay, ay, my hearty, I'll put her through, and you too," replied the young boatman, as he shook out the sail, and hauled the sheet home.

As she felt the strong blast, the old boat lay down before it, and a large wave broke over her gunnel; but Paul luffed her up, so that she did not fill. Whatever Thomas thought of this stirring experience, he kept his seat upon the weather side, and appeared to be perfectly unconcerned. As they came out from under the bluff, where the windows of the house above commanded a

view of their position, they were discovered by
Mrs. Duncan, who again hastened to the beach to
repeat her command more imperatively than before. Paul had steeled his heart to do wrong in
this instance, and he pretended not to see or
hear her; and the boat dashed on her course.

CHAPTER II.

PAUL IS COOL AND SELF-POSSESSED.

BAYVILLE is situated about seven or eight miles from Boston, on the line of one of the principal railroads. A large portion of the inhabitants, even at the time of which I write, were gentlemen doing business in the city, though the place had a ship-yard and several wharves from which the surrounding country was supplied with wood, coal, and lumber. The town is located on both sides of Tenean River, the estuary of which forms a very good harbor, though the place has not yet attained to any considerable commercial importance.

The ship-yard and the wharves were on the north side of the river, which was known as Mercantile Point. On the south side a peninsula extended about half a mile out into the sea,

3

at the extremity of which was the little cottage of Mr. Duncan, the ship carpenter. It was built upon the high bluff, and below it was the beach which had been formed by the continued caving of the earth from the high bank. The cottage was over a mile from the ship-yard, by the road, and not more than half the distance in a straight line across the water. As an easy and pleasant way to get to his work, Mr. Duncan had purchased the old boat, in which Paul had just embarked, for a few dollars, and in good weather generally went over to the ship-yard by water. He was a skilful boatman, and under his tuition his son had learned all the mysteries of sailing a boat. Like most boys, he was disposed to be more daring than was necessary, and it was often that his father and mother found occasion to check him in the pursuit of bold enterprises. Paul was passionately fond of the water, and was proud of his nautical skill and knowledge.

Aquatic sports were all the rage at Bayville, and there were very few gentlemen who had the means that did not own boats of some kind. In the summer season the harbor always presented a brilliant display of yachts, sail boats, and wherries. The largest of these was ·the Flyaway, a splendid yacht of fifty-two tons, which was jointly owned by Major Nettle and Captain Littleton. Even the boys of the High School had a club boat, which, in the warm season, not only afforded them fine sport, but plenty of healthy exercise for the proper development of their physical organization.

On the first day of May, when our story opens, the scholars of the High School had a picnic at Tenean Point, and the boat club had gone down to participate in the festivities of the occasion. Thomas Nettle had been to the city in the morning, and had not returned in season to go down with the club, of which he was a member. It was four miles to the Point by the road, and only half that distance by water, when the wind permitted the passage in a straight line. He did not like the idea of walking so far, choosing rather to incur the danger of being drowned by the upsetting of Paul's old boat.

In spite of the strong wind and the heavy sea, Paul kept ·the boat on her course, though, as the tide was against her, she did not make much headway.

"Can you weather South Point, Paul?" asked Thomas, who had been silent for some time.

"I'm afraid I can't; this old boat makes about as much leeway as headway."

"It is pretty rough out here — isn't it?"

"Rather," replied Paul, indifferently.

"She takes in a good deal of water."

"Mostly spray; you can bale her out, if you have a mind to do so."

Thomas was glad to have something in the shape of occupation, for it required all his power to conceal a certain nervousness, which he would not have had Paul see for all the world. He took the tin kettle, and worked as though the safety of the craft depended entirely upon his efforts.

The wind seemed to increase rather than diminish

in force, and the sail was becoming more exciting every moment; but Paul maintained his self-possession, and though he had some doubts about his ability to keep the old craft right side up, he did not permit his companion to know that he had a single misgiving.

"We can't fetch by the Point," said he, when Thomas had done baling.

"Better come about then; we may get ashore on the rocks."

"Good!" exclaimed Paul, with a hearty laugh.

"What is the matter now?" demanded Thomas.

"The idea of striking a rock on the weather side!" laughed Paul.

"You are right; I didn't think."

The boat now came into comparatively still water, under the lee of Long Island, as the outermost of three small islets, extending out in a line from the mouth of the river, was called. The island was a mass of rocks, rising from ten to twenty feet above high water mark, and as they got behind it, they were sheltered from the

3 *

force of the wind. In this situation, Paul at-
tempted to tack; but the old boat would not
come round in stays, for she had partially lost
her headway, and the tide was against her.

" That's bad," said Thomas; " we shall lose
all we have gained by this."

" Take an oar and heave her head round,
then," replied Paul.

" Ay, ay; " and Thomas took the oar, and
brought her head up to the wind.

There was a coolness and self-possession in the
demeanor of Paul which filled his companion
with confidence as well as admiration, though he
was in no humor to acknowledge it. If Thomas
was not actually terrified by the sweeping billows
and the rude pitching of the boat, it was only
because he felt that he was in the charge of a
skilful boatman. The old craft soon caught the
wind on the other tack, and drove out among the
big waves again.

Paul's mother was still on the beach watching
the uneasy movements of the boat, and in mo-

mentary expectation that she, would be swamped. Her earnest gestures were disregarded by her son, and she was prepared for the worst fate that could befall him. Paul tried to keep his eyes away from her; but he could not help stealing an occasional glance at her, though his conscience reproached him for the pain and terror he was giving her. But he felt that his courage and his reputation as a boatman were at stake, and that, if he failed to achieve the purpose before him, he would be the derision of Thomas Nettle and all his companions.

For two hours the boat labored heavily in the rough sea, and had accomplished about two thirds of the distance to Tenean Point. The young adventurers were now in the worst place in the bay, and the boat was exposed to the full force of the wind and the sea, from which they had before been partially protected by an island.

"What do you think, Paul?" said Thomas, suspending for a moment the work of baling, in which he had been engaged for the last hour.

"What do I think?" replied Paul, coolly, as he wiped the spray from his eyes; "I think it blows tremendous hard."

"So do I."

"Then we shan't quarrel about that, any how."

"Do you think you can make the Point?"

"Certainly I do; I'm in for it, at any rate."

"We don't make much headway."

"That's true."

"I shan't get to the picnic in any kind of season," continued Thomas, crouching down under the weather rail, as a huge wave gave the boat a slap that made her quiver like a leaf.

"I can't help that, Tom; I didn't want you to come this way."

"Don't you think we had better run for the shore, and give it up?"

"I don't think any such thing. If the old boat will only hold together long enough, I'll put you ashore on Tenean Point."

"I'm afraid she won't hold together much longer."

"No matter; we will go it while she does hold together. Can you swim, Tom?"

"You know very well I can swim, Paul."

"Better get your boots off, then."

"Who do you suppose could swim ashore in such a sea as this? Besides, it is over a half a mile, and the surf on the beach would tear a fellow all to pieces."

"You ought to have thought of these things before you came out here."

"It is a great deal worse than I had any idea of," answered Thomas, who had proceeded far enough to be willing to yield a point. "For my part, I am willing to be landed here;" and he pointed to a little cove on the Tenean shore.

"You don't say you have got enough of it, Tom," said Paul, with a smile.

"Enough of it! I want to get to the picnic some time to-day. I hope you don't think I am frightened."

"Of course I don't; you daresn't be frightened after all your big talk before we came out."

"I'll give up on that, Paul. You are the spunkiest fellow with a boat I ever saw. I am willing to say that and stick to it."

"That's saying a good deal."

"But you mustn't suppose I am afraid."

"Of course not; you're only in a hurry to get to the picnic; that's the idea."

"That's just it, and if you will put me ashore at the cove, I will be just as much obliged to you as though you carried me all the way to the Point."

"Let's not back out, Tom."

"I don't back out; and I'm sure you don't."

"It looks a little like backing out to give up the chase."

"You ought to be satisfied, if I am."

"I shan't be satisfied till I land you at the Point."

"Come, come, Paul, don't carry the joke too far. The sea is getting heavier and heavier, and the wind blows a young hurricane."

"O, well, if you really want to back out, I'm willing."

" I don't want to do any thing of the sort. If
you think I can't stand it as long as you can,
you are mistaken," replied Thomas, proudly; and
taking the dipper, he continued to bale out the
water, whistling an air to indicate his indifference
to the perils that surrounded them.

" Put her through, then; we shan't be much
longer, if we don't get swamped."

The boat was now standing out from the shore,
and while Thomas was still busy, whistling off
his fears, a violent gust of wind struck the sail,
causing the boat to heel over so far that she
drank up several buckets of water, and would
have filled if the sprit had not broken, thus re-
moving the pressure.

"Come, Paul, I have got enough of this," cried
Thomas, uneasily.

"I don't think you will be able to get any
more of it, for the sprit has snapped, and we
can't carry sail any longer," replied Paul, apparently unmoved by the accident. " Bale her out
as fast as you can, and I will take an oar,
and keep her head up to the sea."

"What will you do now?" asked Thomas, whose courage was sorely tried by the perilous situation of the boat.

"Get the water out, and we will see what can be done," answered Paul, who, though he had already decided this important question, would not permit his passenger to enter into his counsels, preferring to tantalize him by his mysterious manner.

"Let us get ashore, Paul, as soon as possible."

"Going to back out?"

"No; what's the use of talking in that way, about backing out, when you can't carry sail?" replied Thomas, whose pride was still unconquered, though his courage was rapidly failing him.

"I shall rig a new sprit; there's the boat-hook, which will make a very good one; it is just the right length."

"I'll give up then, and back out," said Thomas, despairing of any relief from the misfortunes that had befallen the boat.

"Don't back out on my account; I will put you ashore at the Point, if you say the word," replied Paul, satisfied now that he had kept his promise and given his friend enough of it.

"Run for the shore, Paul."

"Just as you say;" and the boatman, proud of the triumph he had won over his boastful companion, turned the boat's head towards the shore.

The corner of the sail hung down for the want of a sprit to support it, but as they had the wind free, there was canvas enough to drive her rapidly towards the shore. While they were still half a mile from the cove, Thomas called Paul's attention to a horse and chaise on the beach, from which a man was making violent gestures for them to come ashore.

4

CHAPTER III.

PAUL HEARS BAD NEWS.

"Who is it, Tom?" asked Paul, very anxiously.

"I don't know; can't make him out."

"What can he want with us?"

"Perhaps your mother has sent him after her runaway boy; but whoever ho is, I will tell him you are a fellow of the right spunk."

"Who can it be?"

"What matter who it is? Your mother won't whip you — will she?"

"No, of course not. My mother don't whip me."

"I thought she did, you seem so much afraid of her."

"I am not afraid of her."

"If you are, there is nothing else that can frighten you."

"I mind my mother because she is my mother; because I like to do so, and not because I am afraid of her. You had better not say much more about being afraid, Tom."

"Do you mean to say I was afraid?" said Thomas, smartly.

"If you wasn't afraid, you was confoundedly scared," replied Paul, whose paradox was fully appreciated by his companion.

"Look here, Paul; are you going to tell the fellows that I was scared?" demanded Thomas, rather in a beseeching than an intimidating tone.

"That will depend on circumstances."

"What circumstances?"

"You may as well understand me first as last. You keep talking about my being afraid of my mother, and all that sort of stuff. I'm not afraid of her, and I don't like to be told that I am."

"I won't say it again, then."

"Fellows that live in glass houses mustn't throw stones."

"Do you really think I was frightened, Paul?"

"I really think you was. Didn't you back out?"

"Not till the sail broke down."

"I offered to fix that."

"It's no use to risk a fellow's life for nothing."

"That's the point exactly. Don't you say a word about my mother, and you may talk as big as you please about this scrape."

"I'm not going to talk big about it. I shall give you all the credit you deserve."

"Of course you will. The fellow that holds the bag can let the cat out when he chooses. I don't like to have my mother spoken of as you speak of your mother. She's my mother, and she has always been a good mother to me, and I would do any thing in the world for her. There's only one thing about this scrape that I'm sorry for; and that is, that I didn't mind her. It makes me feel bad."

"She won't say much to you; she will be so

glad to have you safely home, that she won't feel like jawing you," answered Thomas, in what he intended for words of consolation, but which were really heartless and offensive to the penitent.

" My mother don't jaw; it will make her feel bad that I didn't mind her; and that is ten times worse than a scolding or a whipping. — That man keeps shaking his hat to us. Who do you think it is?"

" It looks like Captain Littleton."

" What can he want of me?" said Paul, anxiously.

" If it is Captain Littleton, it is more like he wants me."

In a few moments more the boat darted into the cove, and the boys recognized Captain Littleton in the gentleman who had been beckoning to them.

" Come ashore, Paul, as quick as you can!" shouted he, as he jumped into his chaise, and drove nearer to the point where the boat was to land.

" Do you want me, sir?" asked Paul.

" Yes; you are wanted at home."

4 *

Our hero was filled with terror and anxiety by this reply. He was sure that something had happened, or a gentleman like Captain Littleton would not have taken the trouble to come after him. As the boat struck the bank, he brailed up the sail, and jumped ashore with the painter in his hand.

"Come, Paul, never mind the boat; Thomas will take care of her. Get into the chaise with me as quick as you can," said Captain Littleton.

"What is the matter, sir? What has happened?" demanded Paul, trembling with the most painful solicitude.

"Get into the chaise first, and I will tell you as we return."

"Has any thing happened to my mother, sir?" cried Paul, the tears rushing to his eyes.

"Nothing has happened to your mother, Paul. She is quite well," answered Captain Littleton, as he urged the horse to his utmost speed.

Paul was greatly relieved by this assurance, though it was still evident from the manner of the gentleman, and the speed at which he drove the horse, that some dreadful event had occurred. His conscience smote him for his disobedience to his mother, and he was not in a fit moral condition to meet the shock of adversity with courage and fortitude. He would have given the world, in that anxious moment, to have undone the work of the last three hours, and effaced their record from his conscience.

"Tell me what has happened, if you please, sir," he continued. "Is any of the folks dead? You say it is not my mother."

"Your mother is quite well, and none of your family are dead, though ———."

Captain Littleton paused, and looked at the boy's face, which was still bathed in tears. He saw the misery that he was enduring, and he hesitated to utter words which he knew must carry grief and woe to his heart.

"You must be calm and firm, Paul," continued the kind gentleman. "It is not so bad as you suppose, and we may hope for the best. Your father has just met with a serious accident."

"Is he dead, sir?" gasped Paul. "You don't tell me the whole story, sir."

"He is not dead, Paul; but he is very badly hurt."

"He is alive, then?"

"He is."

Paul closely scrutinized the expression of Captain Littleton, fearful that he had not told him the whole truth.

"Are you sure he was not killed?" he asked, still unsatisfied.

"He was alive when I left him, but that was nearly an hour ago."

"I am thankful if he is alive. How did it happen, sir?"

"He fell from the bow of the ship upon which he was at work, and struck a pile of timber. I am afraid he is very badly hurt. I happened to be near the ship-yard at the time, and assisted in carrying him home. He is conscious, and asked for you. Your mother said you were out in the boat."

Paul burst into tears again at these words, for he realized the nature and depth of his mother's feelings when she-had uttered them, and how bitterly did he regret his act of disobedience! The dreadful event had come to intensify the anguish of his penitence, and he felt that, if he had not done wrong, he could have met the calamity with patience and resolution. When children do wrong, they know not what event may occur to increase a thousand fold the bitterness of their remorse.

" Do you think my father is alive now ? " sobbed Paul.

" I hope so; but it is impossible to foretell the result. The doctors spoke very despondingly of his case; but we must hope for the best."

" How does my mother bear it ? "

" As well as could be expected, considering the suddenness of the calamity."

" O, it will kill her," groaned Paul.

" I hope not; you must be calm, my boy. It is dreadful, I know; but we must not add to the pain of the sufferer by useless lamentation."

"I will be as calm as I can, sir; but it is awful to have such a thing happen just now."

"We know not what a day or an hour may bring forth, Paul."

"Yes, but to have it happen now! If it had been at any other time, I could have borne it better," continued the penitent boy, wiping away the tears that blinded him.

"We cannot choose the time for such an event to happen."

"If it had only come before I left home! O, dear."

"Be calm, Paul; we could not select a time when we should be prepared for such a calamity. You must not suppose one time is better than another for trials and sorrows."

"You do not understand me, Captain Little-ton," replied Paul, earnestly. "I disobeyed my mother in going out in the boat. She told me to come ashore, and stood on the beach beckoning and calling to me not to go, but I didn't mind her. That's what makes me feel so bad about it."

"I am sorry you disobeyed her, for you must suffer the more for your disobedience."

"I was sorry I did so before I came ashore, and now I would give all the world if I had minded mother, and let Tom Nettle laugh at me as much as he pleased."

"Tom is a wild boy, and you must not heed his jeers."

"I will not, another time. You think my father is not dead?"

"I think not," replied Captain Littleton, as he increased the speed of the horse.

Paul did not say much more, but wept in silence as the chaise dashed along the road. Every moment seemed like an hour, till he came in sight of the cottage of his father. There were the two sulkies of the doctors, and a crowd of people at the gate, to enable him to realize the dreadful calamity which had overtaken him. The panting horse stopped before the door, and Paul's limbs almost failed him, as he dragged himself into the house.

"O Paul," sobbed his mother, who met him at the door, "I thought you would never come. I'm afraid you won't have a father a great while longer."

"Forgive me, mother, for what I did," cried Paul.

"I do forgive you, my son; but come, your poor father wants to see you very much."

His mother took him by the hand, and led him into the chamber where his father lay. He was shocked by the change which a few short hours had produced, and he needed not the skill of the physicians to assure him that Mr. Duncan had but a short time to live.

"Paul," said his father, faintly, "I shall soon be no more, and I leave your mother and your brothers and sisters to your care. Take good care of them, Paul, for they will soon have no one else to help them. Be a good boy, and be an honest man, and every thing will go well with you. Be true to your God and true to yourself, and then all the world cannot harm you. May God keep you in the path of duty as long as you live."

Mr. Duncan closed his eyes with an audible sigh, and Paul burst into tears, realizing that he was about to lose the kindest and best of fathers.

"Don't cry, my boy," said the sufferer; "be a man, and in a little while the struggle will be over with me."

The whole family were gathered round the bed, and Mr. Duncan gave them his blessing, for the doctors assured him his hour was at hand. We will not dwell upon the painful scene. In an hour all was still in that room save the sobs of the bereaved widow, who stood gazing in agony upon the silent form which she had seen go out from her that morning in the full vigor of health and strength. The angel of death was there, and had done his work.

Paul was stupefied by the suddenness of the shock, and all the currents of his existence seemed to stop in their flow. He spent the afternoon in his chamber, trying to understand the nature of his situation. He had dried his tears, but the deeper grief had gone in upon his heart. He spent a wakeful night in thinking of the past, and in endeavoring to make himself believe that his father was dead. All that he had ever done for him, all that he had ever said to him, came up before him with a vividness that made them seem like realities.

In this condition he moved about the house till after the funeral, mechanically executing such duties as he was required to perform; but every thing was so unnatural to him that he could hardly persuade himself of the reality of his being. The death of his father was an epoch in his existence, a turning point in his career, and the wheels of time, the current of events, stopped, soon to resume their course in a different direction.

When the last rites of love and respect had been paid to the remains of his father, Paul roused himself from his stupor, and began to examine the future. At the death bed of his parent he had received a solemn charge, and he carefully reviewed the words, and recalled the expression with which it had been committed to him. His mother and his brothers and sisters had been given into his care, and he felt the responsibility of the position he had accepted. He determined, to the best of his ability, to discharge his duty to them; but he was sorely troubled to think of some way by which he could earn money enough to support them, for he had put a literal construction upon the dying words of his father.

CHAPTER IV.

PAUL BECOMES THE HEAD OF THE FAMILY.

For a week after the funeral Paul racked his brain in devising expedients to supply the place of his father in a pecuniary point of view, but without success. If he went into a store, or obtained such a place as a boy can fill, it would pay him only two or three dollars a week, and this would be scarcely any thing towards the support of the family, for his father had generally earned twelve dollars a week during the greater portion of the year. He wanted to do something better. He did not expect to make so much as his father had made, but was determined, if possible, to earn at least half as much.

Thus far his reflection had been to little purpose, for it was no small matter for a boy to charge himself with double the work of one of his age.

He had not yet consulted his mother, nor obtained her views in regard to the support of the family. He did not know whether she expected him to do the whole of it, but it did not appear reasonable to him that she could do any thing more than to keep house and take care of the children. He wished that he could go to her and relieve her of all responsibility in regard to the money affairs, and let her live just as she had been accustomed to live before the death of his father; and he almost cried with vexation, after he had vainly ransacked his brains for the means, to think he could not do so. He could not hit upon any plan that would meet his expectations, and he decided to have a talk with her in relation to the future.

"What are we going to do, mother?" he asked, as he seated himself in the kitchen where Mrs. Duncan was getting supper.

"That is what I have been thinking of myself," she replied. "I have been talking with Captain Littleton to-day, and he gave me some good advice, and offered me any assistance I might require."

5 *

"You surely don't mean to live on charity, mother," added Paul, proudly.

"Certainly not. Captain Littleton did not offer to give me any thing; only to assist me in getting work for myself and you."

"O, well, that's all right."

"While we have our health and strength, we shall not have to ask other help of any one."

"Of course not."

"I hope I am above asking charity, or taking it either."

"I knew you were. What did Captain Littleton say?"

"Thanks to the goodness and forethought of your father, we are not left entirely destitute," replied Mrs. Duncan, wiping a tear from her cheek.

"I didn't know there was any thing left."

"After paying all the funeral expenses and the doctors' bills, I shall have fifty dollars in money. Your father had no debts."

"Fifty dollars isn't much, mother, towards supporting the family. It wouldn't last two months."

"That is very true; we have more than that. Three years ago your father had his life insured for a thousand dollars, and this sum will be paid to me in a few days."

"I didn't know that," said Paul, greatly surprised to find they had what seemed to him so vast a sum. "We shall get along very well."

"Your father used to calculate that it cost him about eight dollars a week to live, or about four hundred dollars a year. If he had had work all the year round, he might have saved a very handsome sum, he used to tell me."

"It will not cost us eight dollars a week now."

"No; we must live very prudently; but if it cost us only five, a thousand dollars would last but a few years, and what should we do then?"

"We must not spend it then."

"Captain Littleton told me what he thought we had better do. This house in which we live can be bought for fifteen hundred dollars, though the owner has always asked eighteen hundred, and ——."

"You don't really think of such a thing as buying the house?" interrupted Paul, filled with amazement at the magnitude of the idea.

"That is what Captain Littleton advises me to do."

"But you haven't money enough."

"I can give a mortgage for five hundred dollars. The rent of the house is one hundred and forty dollars, and Mr. Freeman says he cannot afford to let it for any less. Now, if we buy it, we can pay a thousand dollars down, and we shall owe five hundred, on which we shall have to pay the interest, amounting to thirty dollars. By this plan, we should have to pay out only about fifty dollars a year for interest and taxes, or about a dollar a week. In this way we can get along on five dollars a week."

"Buy the house then, by all means, mother. Five dollars a week! Well, I think I shall be able to support the family, after all."

"You, Paul?" exclaimed Mrs. Duncan, with a smile.

"I am sure I can."

"What do you intend to do?"

"I don't know yet."

"Your poor father intended that you should enter the High School this fall; but I suppose that cannot be. Captain Littleton said he would get you a place where you could have two or three dollars a week."

"I must make more than that, mother," replied Paul, shaking his head.

"You must not be too ambitious. If you get two or three dollars a week, you will do very well, and that sum will be a great help to me."

"You heard what father said to me in his last moments?" said Paul, with solemn earnestness. "He told me to take care of my mother and of my brothers and sisters, and I mean to do so."

"But he never had a thought that you could earn money enough to support the whole of us. You are a good boy, Paul, but you must not try to do too much."

"If we can live on five dollars a week, I am almost sure I can earn that."

"That is a good deal for a boy like you."

"I can do it, I know."

"Captain Littleton said he would find a place for you."

"I shall be very much obliged to him, and will take any place I can get; but I am certain before long that I can make five dollars a week."

"Don't think of such a thing. There are a great many men who get no more than that. You must work your way up, little by little, Paul, and one of these days you will obtain a good situation."

"That's just what I mean to do. Little by little — that's my motto; and if I can only get hold any where, you may leave the rest to me."

"You are a good boy, Paul, and you will succeed by and by," said Mrs. Duncan, proudly. "I expect to get some work myself next week, and I have no doubt we shall do very well."

" What work, mother ? " asked Paul, a shadow
of dissatisfaction passing over his face.

" Captain Littleton thought he could get me a
chance to make bags for the flour mills."

" I don't mean to have you take in work,
mother. You have enough to do to take care of
the house and the children."

" I can do a good deal besides. Sarah can
help a great deal about the house, and with what
we can all do, we shall get along very well indeed. We ought to be very thankful for all the
blessings that surround us."

" We are enough sight better off than I thought,"
replied Paul; " but I don't want to have you
make a slave of yourself. You used to work
hard enough ; and now, if you are going to take in
work, you will wear yourself out in a few years."

" I guess not, Paul. There is somebody knock-
ing at the door; go and see who it is."

Paul went to the door, and the visitor proved
to be Captain Littleton.

" I was looking for you, Paul," said he. " I'm

going to give a dinner party to-morrow, and I
want a mess of perch, fresh from the rocks, by
twelve o'clock. I want you should go down and
catch them for me. You always have good luck
at fishing. Will you do this for me, Paul?"

"Yes, sir; certainly I will."

"I will speak to your mother about it."

Paul conducted Captain Littleton into the little
parlor, and called his mother. She was willing
that he should go, and glad to have him do
something in return for the gentleman's repeated
acts of kindness.

"I will give you twenty cents a dozen for
them, Paul, and I want at least five dozen," continued the captain.

"He will not charge any thing, sir," added
Mrs. Duncan."

"Not a cent, sir," repeated Paul.

"It's a fair trade, young man, and I won't take
them unless I pay for them."

"I don't want any pay from you, sir."

"But I choose to pay you, and you must take

your orders from me in this instance. Have you any clams for bait?"

"No, sir. I will get some to-night."

"Very well; you may go and get them now, and I will talk to your mother about business."

Paul took his hat and went down to the beach. Embarking in the old boat, he sailed over to Tencan, where plenty of clams were to be had, and a bucket full was soon procured. Like a prudent fisherman, he made all his arrangements for the next day. First he repaired the worn-out sail, then made a new sprit, and refitted the tiller to the rudder head. When every thing was in ship-shape order about the boat, he took out his perch lines, ganged on a new hook, and rigged an extra sinker for use in case of accident.

"Going a fishing, Paul?" said John Duncan, his brother, a lad of ten, who joined him when he had nearly completed his preparations.

"I'm going down in the morning to get a mess of perch for Captain Littleton."

6

"Let me go with you, Paul?"

"You must go to school."

"It don't keep."

"Ask mother, then; if she is willing, I am."

"Have you got a line for me?"

"Yes."

John Duncan, for his years, was almost as much of a sailor and fisherman as Paul. Both of them took to the water like ducks, and seemed to understand all about a boat as if by instinct. The prospect of a day down below fired the imagination of the "young salt," and he ran up the bluff with all his might to obtain the desired permission.

"May I go a-fishing with Paul to-morrow, mother?" shouted he, as he rushed into the parlor, without noticing the presence of Captain Littleton.

"We will see about that by and by. Take off your cap."

"How do you do, John?" said Captain Littleton.

"Pretty well," replied John, whose head keeled over on the port side, as he discovered the visitor, and three fingers found their way into his mouth.

"You want to go a-fishing, do you?"

"Yes, sir."

"Do you think it is safe to let him go?" asked Mrs. Duncan.

"I ain't afraid, mother," interrupted the young hopeful.

"I know you are not, and that's one reason why I don't like to trust you in the boat."

"Your boys take to the water in a natural way; and when boys have a decided taste of that kind, it isn't of much use to thwart them."

"I know it isn't; but John has worried my life out since he was four years old, for he is always in the water."

"I should use proper precaution with him; but Paul is so good a boatman that I should not be afraid to trust him in his care."

"You may go, John," added Mrs. Duncan. "I have almost made up my mind to let him live in the water; but I can't help going to the window when he is out on the beach, at least twenty times a day, to see if he isn't in trouble."

"To return to Paul," said Captain Littleton, resuming the remarks which the entrance of John had interrupted. "I have the refusal of a place in a lawyer's office, where the salary is two dollars and a half a week. It is small pay, but it is better than nothing."

"He expects more than that. It would have astonished you to hear him talk a little while ago. He is going to assume the whole burden of supporting the family, and is not willing that I should do any thing."

"He is a smart boy, and ought to have a good place."

"He says he means to make five dollars a week; but that is mere boy-talk."

"I like his spirit, but he will hardly be expected to earn five dollars a week at present. I hope I shall be able to find him a better place than the one I spoke of."

"You are very good, sir; I shall never be able to repay you for your kindness."

"Don't mention it, ma'am. I am very glad to do any thing I can for you. You have made up your mind then to purchase the house?"

"Yes, sir."

"I think that's the best thing you can do under the circumstances. The property is rising in value, and in a few years, if you should want to sell, it would bring two thousand dollars. I will see Freeman as I return, and the papers shall be made out immediately."

"Thank you, sir."

Captain Littleton took his leave, and Mrs. Duncan was very grateful to him for the friendly interest he manifested in her affairs. When Paul returned to the house, his mother informed him that her friend had found a place for him; but the young aspirant had got an idea, and made up his mind to decline the situation.

6 *

CHAPTER V.

PAUL COOKS HIS OWN BREAKFAST, AND GOES
A FISHING.

ABOUT six miles east of Bayville was a rocky island, around which perch were abundant. Paul had often been there with his father, and was familiar with the locality. He knew just where to moor his boat to have good luck in fishing, and was acquainted with all the channels, currents, and bars in the bay. He was not only a skilful seaman, but a good pilot, and felt as much at home on the bay as in the streets of Bayville.

It would be low tide in the bay at seven o'clock, and Paul made his calculations accordingly. The best time to fish was on the "young flood," or soon after the tide had turned to come in; and, if the wind should happen to be light or contrary, it would take him a long time to run down to Rock Island, as the place was called; therefore he must go down with the tide. To accomplish his purpose it was necessary that he should start by five o'clock in the morning, which was an hour before his usual breakfast time.

He did not sleep very well that night, for the great idea to which we have alluded was creating an immense commotion in his mind. He had reasoned out the certainty of his being able to support the family, and he felt as proud of his great resolution as though he had achieved its full fruits. When, at last, he dropped asleep, it was only to dream of great speculations, and of the satisfaction he should have in giving his mother money enough on Saturday night to pay all the expenses of the family for a week.

He woke very early in the morning, and as he jumped out of bed he heard the clock on the Town Hall strike four. He did not mean to disturb his mother, and therefore cautioned John not to make any noise. He was not like some boys, who growl and grumble at their mothers if their meals are not ready when they want them. Stealing softly down stairs, he went to the back kitchen, and made a fire in the stove.

"Now, John, you go down to the boat, and bale her out," said he to his brother, as the latter joined him.

"Are you going without any breakfast?" asked John.

"No; breakfast will be ready by the time you have baled out the boat."

"You haven't called mother yet?"

"I don't mean to do so."

"Where will you get your breakfast, then?"

"I will get it myself."

"You don't know how to cook," replied John, incredulously.

"You see if I don't; now go ahead, and don't make a noise, or you will wake mother."

Paul then went down cellar, and brought up a few potatoes, which he washed and put into the kettle. A piece of pork and a slice of veal were deposited in the frying pan, ready to be cooked at the proper time. The coffee, not omitting the important bit of fish skin, was put in the coffee-pot, and operations in that quarter were suspended till the water in the tea-kettle should boil. Though our hero had never actually performed these manœuvres with his own hands, he had seen them executed so many times that he was perfectly familiar with the routine.

Every thing upon the stove was doing very well, and he pulled out the table, which he proceeded to cover with the proper articles for the morning meal. Each article was carefully disposed in its proper place, for Paul had already learned that food tastes better in the midst of order and neatness, than when taken in dirt and confusion. It is true, he made some mistakes for the want of experience, and was frequently obliged to stop and think what articles were required; but when the table was set, he was satisfied with its cheerful and neat appearance. By this time the tea-kettle was spouting out long jets of steam, and the lid was rattling under the influence

of the commotion beneath it. Paul poured a little of the boiling water into the coffee-pot, and
then came an appalling difficulty — he did not
know how much to put in, and was not sure that
he had taken the proper quantity of coffee. At a
venture he filled the pot half full, and then proceeded to cook the meat. After the coffee had
boiled ten or fifteen minutes, he tested its strength,
and added more water. He was delighted with
his success, and when John returned from the
beach, he was putting the breakfast upon the
table.

"Breakfast is ready," said Paul.

"Did you cook it, though?"

"I did; I told you I could."

"I'll give up now. Why don't you hire out
for a cook?"

"Perhaps I shall, one of these days."

"Wouldn't mother's eyes stick out if she should
happen in about this time!"

"I guess not much."

But they did, for just as the boys were seating

themselves at the table, Mrs. Duncan entered the
room.

"Why, boys! what have you been doing?"
exclaimed she, astonished at the regularity with
which every thing seemed to be proceeding in her
absence.

"Only getting something to eat before we go,"
replied Paul.

"Why didn't you call me?"

"I thought I wouldn't get you up so early;
besides, I could get breakfast just as well myself."

"I declare you are a good cook, Paul. Your
potatoes and meat look as nice as can be. How is
your coffee? Did you put a piece of fish-skin in
the pot?"

"Yes, ma'am."

"Did you put any salt on the meat?"

"I did; come, mother, sit down and eat your
breakfast."

Mrs. Duncan accepted this polite invitation, and
seating herself in her accustomed place, began to

pour out the coffee. It was clear, and of the right strength, and she liberally praised Paul for his culinary skill, and declared that her son was a jewel about the house. The breakfast seemed even better than usual that morning, and our hero was as proud as though he had built a meeting house.

"Come, John, we must bear a hand; there isn't a breath of wind, and it will take us some time to make Rock Island," said Paul, as he rose from the table. "Have you filled the jug with water?"

"No, but I will."

"Here is some gingerbread and cheese for luncheon," added Mrs. Duncan, as she handed Paul a basket she had filled for their use. "Now, be very careful, and don't run any risk. Look out for squalls, and don't carry sail too long."·

"I'll be very careful, mother. You may trust me to go round the world," replied Paul.

"But I wish you had a better boat."

"She'll do very well, mother, though I hope to have a better one some time or other."

The jug was filled at the pump, and with their provisions and water the boys set off with light hearts for the work of the day.

Paul felt the responsibility of the trust which Captain Littleton had imposed upon him. He was going to make some money by the operation, and upon this day's success depended the hopes which he had been cherishing in régard to his new scheme.

There are always some drawbacks to disturb the best-laid plans, and when Paul reached the bluff, he discovered the boat adrift at some distance from the shore.

"You are a careless fellow, John," he cried. "You didn't make fast the boat."

"That's too bad, Paul; I didn't mean to do that," replied John, vexed at the accident.

"I don't suppose you did; but you are careless."

"I thought I made her fast. What shall we do, Paul? I would rather given any thing than had this happen."

7

"So would I; but there is no use of crying about it. There isn't a skiff within half a mile of here."

"I'll tell you what I'll do, Paul," said John, putting down the jug and throwing off his jacket. "I'll swim out to her and scull her in."

Paul made no objection to this plan, and in half a minute more, John had stripped and was swimming with all his might after the boat, which was perhaps fifty rods from the shore. He was a vigorous swimmer, as self-possessed in the water as on the land, and his brother had no fears in regard to his safety, or his ability to reach the boat.

It did not take the little fellow long to catch the boat, and the accident did not make more than half an hour's delay. The stores were taken on board, and before John had time to dress himself, the boat was under sail, and working slowly down the bay. A light breeze from the west had sprung up, and a gentle ripple at the bow assured the young fishermen that every thing was progressing in a satisfactory manner.

" I should like to be a fisherman, Paul," said John, who sat on the bottom of the boat opening clams for bait.

" Perhaps you may be one of these days," replied Paul, moodily. " I think I shall do something in that line right off."

" You, Paul?"

" Yes, but don't you say a word about it to anybody, above all, not to mother. I have been thinking about it all night."

" What do you mean, Paul?"

The ambitious youth had a great idea in his mind, which was struggling to be actualized. More than twenty times since the preceding evening had the words of Captain Littleton crossed his imagination, and kindled up a great blaze of possibilities and probabilities. " I will give you twenty cents a dozen for them," the captain had said. If he would buy perch, others would buy them. He had a boat, and there would not be many days when he could not catch as many as five or six dozen. Even at a shilling a dozen he could make a dollar a day.

This was his scheme — to supply Bayville with fresh fish. He had as good a chance to sell them as the men who went through the place blowing their tin horns. He should have an advantage over them, for his fish were certain to be fresh, and he was sure the people would be willing to patronize him. The plan promised exceedingly well, and he wished to talk it over with some one, though he was not quite ready to have it made public. It was true, John was only ten years old, and didn't know much; but he wanted to talk with somebody about it, and so he concluded to take his brother into his confidence.

"What do I mean, John?" said he. "Why can't I catch perch every day, and sell them in town?"

"Sure enough, why can't you?" replied John, delighted with the idea, and perhaps bringing some selfish motives to bear upon it.

"We can haul 'em in as fast as we can throw over the line off the rocks, and there are rich folks enough in Bayville to buy them."

"It's a first-rate idea," exclaimed John, with enthusiasm. "You might go down farther, and catch cod and haddock."

"I would if I had a good boat."

"Father used to go out after cod and haddock in this boat."

"I know, but she is getting rather shaky."

The great idea was discussed in all its bearings till they reached Rock Island, when Paul carefully selected his position, and let go the anchor. The hooks were baited and the lines thrown over, and never before had Paul taken his fishing apparatus when so much seemed to depend upon the success of his efforts. His heart beat as the sinker touched the bottom, and he pulled it up the proper distance. All his fortunes for the future appeared to hang upon the result.

"Hurrah! I've got one!" shouted John, as with childish eagerness he pulled in his line.

It was a sculpin!

Was this a type of his own success? Was he to watch his chance on the great sea of life, and finally, after all his anxious watching and toil, was

7 *

he to pull in only a sculpin? These were painful thoughts to Paul, and his heart almost sunk within him, as he considered the possible failure of his favorite scheme. If he failed in this, he must accept the paltry two dollars and a half a week, and let his mother drudge like a slave. He could not tolerate the thought of failure, and ——

A bite!

Paul did not whistle till he got out of the woods, and announced his success to John by slapping a monster perch upon the bottom of the boat. If that was a type of his success he was satisfied. Before he had time to follow out the reflections suggested by the event, John hauled in the mate to the big fish, and another had taken hold of his own hook.

By ten o'clock there were six dozen perch in the basket, besides three handsome tautog and half a dozen sea flounders. The young fisherman was satisfied, hauled up killock, and made sail for home. His heart was as light as the upper air, and he was confident of the success of his grand scheme.

CHAPTER VI.

PAUL MAKES A GOOD SPECULATION.

"Now, John, you must steer, while I skin the perch," said Paul, as he resigned the helm to his brother.

"That I will," replied he, with alacrity, for he did not often get a chance to handle the boat, and was fond of the amusement.

"But you must be careful, and keep your eyes open, for we have no time to spare," added the youthful skipper.

"Do you think I don't know how to steer a boat?" asked John, hurt by the insinuation.

"You know how well enough, if you will pay attention to it, and not be fooling with her."

"I'll keep her right."

Paul took from under the thwart an old shoe-knife which had been ground down to one third of its original width. It had been well sharpened for this important occasion, but he had provided an old whetstone as a further precaution against a dull blade. To skin a perch neatly and expeditiously is a nice operation; but Paul had had sufficient practice in the art to render him a skilful hand. Seating himself on the lee rail, he commenced work in earnest, occasionally glancing up to see that the boat was doing her best in the way of sailing.

"How much will you make, Paul, if you sell all your fish?" asked John.

"The perch will bring a dollar and twenty cents, if I get twenty cents a dozen for them."

"The tautog are worth something."

"They are worth a quarter apiece."

"You have done a good day's work then?"

"If I sell the fish, I shall," answered Paul, with a smile of satisfaction. "Come, John, the sail is shaking, and you have lost the wind," he added, as his brother carelessly luffed her up.

"I was adding up the perch and the tautog."

" You must mind the boat; you must stop
talking, if you can't do your duty without."

John promised to be more careful, and Paul
had no further occasion to complain of his inat-
tention. The younger fisherman was a good boy,
but he had not yet been trained to that steadi-
ness of purpose which is necessary to success.
He was only ten years old, and it was not to
be expected that he should fully appreciate the
earnestness of his brother's purpose, though he
was beginning to realize that close attention was
necessary in order to accomplish great deeds. He
was fond of trying experiments, just for the fun
of the thing; and when he had been permitted
to take the helm on other occasions, he wanted
to do something besides keep her in a direct
course — to see how close she would lie to the
wind without letting the sail shake, to run down
a floating mass of seaweed, or chase a stick of
wood; but on this trip, he was guilty of no
greater indiscretion than carelessness.

Long before the boat reached Bayville, Paul

had skinned and strung the fish; and their appearance on the line was creditable to his skill. Leaving John to secure the boat, he took the fish and hastened up to the house of Captain Littleton. He found that gentleman in his garden with his guests.

"Well, Paul, what luck?" asked he, as the young fisherman came in sight.

"First-rate, sir."

"How many have you got?"

"Six dozen."

"Just the number I want. Carry them into the kitchen, Paul. I declare, you have dressed them very nicely."

"I tried to have them right, sir, and I am glad they suit you," replied Paul, modestly, as he walked towards the rear of the house.

"Stop, Paul; what have you got there?" said Captain Littleton.

"Tautog, sir; and if you will permit me, I will leave them in the kitchen with the perch."

"You are a lucky fisherman, Paul; those are

handsome fish, and if you will leave them, I will
make it all right when you come out. That is a
luxury I did not expect."

Paul was delighted by the commendation of his
friend, and the splendid scheme of his future operations increased in importance with every word
that was uttered. With a light heart he ran
into the kitchen with his stock, and then returned .
to Captain Littleton.

"Here is two dollars, Paul," said he, handing
him a bill.

"That is too much, sir," stammered Paul, overwhelmed at the idea of having made two dollars
in one day.

"It is right, my boy; take it. You mustn't
be bashful if you are going to fight your way
through the world."

"You are very kind, sir, but this is more than
the fish come to," answered Paul, taking the
bill.

"No, it isn't; the perch come to a dollar
and twenty cents, the tautog to seventy-five,

which make a dollar and ninety-five cents. So we will call it square, and I am very much obliged to you besides."

"I didn't mean to charge you any thing for the tautog, sir."

"Look here, Paul; when you get rich I will accept your gifts; but now, my boy, I will take the will for the deed, and I feel just as grateful to you as though you had presented me a service of plate. You have done well, and I am glad of it."

"Thank you, sir; I am very much obliged to you for this, and for all you have done for my mother," replied Paul, as he put the bank bill in his pocket.

"By the way, how about that place in the lawyer's office, Paul?" said Captain Littleton, as the young fisherman turned to go home.

"If you please, sir, I had rather not take the place."

"You are going to do better, then?"

"Yes, sir, I think I can. I am very much

obliged to you for the trouble you have taken."

"Not at all, my boy; I didn't think the situation would be large enough to suit your ambition. What are you going to do, Paul?"

"I am going to catch fish, and sell them in town, sir," replied Paul, boldly, though he could hardly keep down the emotions that swelled in his bosom.

"Good, my boy! I like an enterprising spirit, and I dare say you will do very well. You may put me down for two dozen perch every Saturday."

"Thank you, sir."

"I will speak to my neighbors, and I have no doubt you will find a market for all the fish you can catch."

"You are very kind."

"What does your mother say about the plan?"

"I haven't told her yet. It is a new idea. I am afraid she will not like it very well."

"She will not object very strongly."

8

" If you would speak to her about it, if you please, sir; she will think every thing of what you say."

" I will, Paul. When you catch any more tautog, be sure and bring them to me."

" I certainly will, Captain Littleton," answered Paul, as he bounded towards home, his heart filled with gratitude to his friend, and with hope for the success of his darling scheme.

Half a dozen times on the way, he put his hand into his pocket to feel of the old black wallet, that contained the proceeds of his first day's work. He had never done a job before which produced more than half a dollar, and the immense sum in his pocket seemed enough to make or break an ordinary bank. Such a run of luck was almost incredible. Wouldn't his mother be astonished when he handed her that two dollar bill!

He had some misgivings in regard to his mother's consent; for like all good mothers, who love their sons, she did not like to have him exposed to danger. But that two dollar bill, and the

brilliant promise of success which the future held
out to him, would be strong arguments in favor
of the scheme, and he hoped to triumph over
every objection she could present.

Before he reached the cottage, Paul contrived to
subdue some of his enthusiasm, and walked into
the kitchen, where his mother was getting dinner,
as coolly and indifferently as though nothing extraordinary had happened. It was hard work for
him to keep down the excitement that was raging
within, but he had determined not to make a fool
of himself.

"Well, Paul, have you had a good time," said
Mrs. Duncan, as he entered the room.

"First-rate, mother," he replied; though he
was not exactly pleased to find that she regarded
the trip to Rock Island in the light of a pleasure
excursion.

"Did you get as many fish as Captain Littleton wanted?"

"Yes, more too; I left six dozen perch and
three handsome tautog in his kitchen just now."

" You were lucky."

" I am good for as many as that every day.
Look here, mother ; " and he pulled out his wal-
let, and took therefrom the two dollar bill.
" What do you think of that ? "

" Did he give you all that ? "

" He did."

" He is very liberal."

" That he is ; but the fish came to about that;
the tautog are worth a quarter apiece."

" You have done bravely, my boy. If you
could make half as much money as that every
day, we should have all we want, and more too."

" I can, mother; and I mean to do so," replied
Paul, thinking this a good opportunity to announce his magnificent intentions.

" You mustn't be too confident, Paul."

" I know I can."

" And, pray, what do you mean to do ? " inquired Mrs. Duncan, with an incredulous smile.

" I am going into the fishing business, mother."

" Into what ? "

" Into the fishing business."

" What in the world do you mean by that? "

" I mean just what I say, mother? "

" Is the boy crazy! " demanded Mrs. Duncan, suspending her culinary operations, and looking with interest into the animated face of her son.

" I am as regular as I ever was in my life. I've thought it all over, and spoken to Captain Littleton besides; and he says go ahead," replied Paul, making an early use of the captain's encouraging words.

" But I don't understand what you mean? Going into the fishing business? "

" Yes, ma'am; we've got a boat, and I mean to go down to Rock Island every day, Sundays excepted, and catch perch. I mean to sell them here in Bayville, and Captain Littleton told me to put him down for two dozen every Saturday. That's the idea, mother."

" But, Paul —— "

" If I can get a shilling a dozen for them, I can make a dollar a day as easy as you can turn

8 *

your hand over," added Paul, who was not disposed to let his mother speak upon impulse.

"You would have to be on the water every day."

"What of that, mother? The water is a good thing to be on, and just as safe as the land, if you are only a mind to think so."

"Rather dangerous, I'm afraid."

"O, no, mother; it's only a notion some folks have, that the water isn't safe."

"Hundreds of people are drowned every year."

"And hundreds smashed up and killed on the railroads. Why, Captain Mitchell don't think it is safe to go about much on the land. He only feels secure when he is in his old whale boat. He won't get into a chaise or a wagon — don't think it is safe to ride in them; but he knocks about the bay in all sorts of weather. Please don't object to it, mother, for I've set my heart upon the business, and I'm satisfied I shall do well," said Paul, with kindling enthusiasm.

"Well, if you are set upon it, I don't want to

say too much against it," replied Mrs. Duncan, doubtfully.

"Captain Littleton will speak to you about it, and he understands these things."

"I know he does; but after all, I would rather have you safe on land."

"I shall be safe enough, mother; and I shall be able to take care of the family without your making bags."

"You are a good boy, Paul," added his mother, turning from him to wipe away the tears that moistened her eyes, for in the loneliness of her widowhood she realized what it was to have such a noble and devoted son.

Paul was delighted to think he had so easily smoothed over matters with her. He had expected to have a hard beat to windward in reconciling her to his plan, but she had proved much more reasonable than he anticipated. He attributed his ready victory in a great measure to the influence of Captain Littleton's name, and he was confident he would remove any remaining doubts she might harbor.

After dinner Paul went up to his room, and taking from his drawer a little account book, which had long been waiting to be used, he entered the amount of the day's sales upon the first page.

"Little by little," said he, as he returned the book to the drawer, "and one of these days I shall be rich."

This was a very comforting reflection, and notwithstanding the possible slip between the cup and the lip, he enjoyed the full benefit of it.

CHAPTER VII.

PAUL GOES INTO BUSINESS ON HIS OWN AC-
COUNT.

BEFORE night, all the arrangements for the next day's trip were completed, and Paul retired at an early hour, so as to be up in season in the morning. The excitement which his great project created in his mind, however, would not let him sleep till he was actually exhausted with thinking. He did not wake till five o'clock in the morning, which made him so ashamed of himself, that he could hardly conceal his vexation, especially as he found his mother was up, and his breakfast was nearly ready, when he went down stairs. But on reflection he found he was early enough, for it would be low tide nearly an hour later than on the preceding day.

While he was eating his breakfast, his brother John came down. It was an unusually early hour

for him to rise, and it was evident from the haste
with which he completed his toilet, after he found
Paul had not gone, that he had an idea of his own,
as well as his brother.

"Mayn't I go with you, Paul?" asked he.

"You must go to school."

"Mayn't I stay away from school to-day, mother?" added he, turning quickly to Mrs. Duncan.

"I'd rather you wouldn't, John."

"Why not, mother?" whined he.

"I don't want you to stay out of school a single
day, when it can be prevented."

"I should think I might go with Paul. I can
catch as many fish as he can."

"Paul is older than you are, and he always
kept close to his school till he left."

"I want to do something towards supporting
the family, as well as he."

Mrs. Duncan laughed, and so did Paul; for however ambitious the young gentleman might have
been to bear his full share of the burden of the
family, it was too evident that his taste for boating

and fishing was the dominant motive for absenting himself from school.

"Let me go with you, Paul."

"Mother says you must go to school, and I think you had better be there."

"Who will steer the boat while you skin the fish?" demanded John, who had a proper idea of the value of his services, and was not at all pleased at the thought of having them undervalued.

"I shall try to get along some way without you. I should like to have you go, first rate, John; but I don't think you ought to stay out of school. You will have a vacation next week, and you may go every day then, if you want to."

"You ought to take me with you, Paul," continued John, resorting to the persuasive, now that the argumentative had failed.

"I tell you I should like to have you go with me, if it were not for your school."

John exhausted his store of arguments and persuasions without effect, and then fled to his room to cry over his defeat. Paul sympathized with his brother in his disappointment, but as the head of the family, he could not, on principle, yield the point. Taking his jug of water and his lunch, he left the house and hastened to the beach. The wind was light, as on the preceding day, and it took him nearly two hours to run down to Rock Island, for the old boat was a very heavy sailer even under the most favorable circumstances.

Paul did not feel quite so nervous as on the day before, for he was so confident of success that he did not feel uneasy even when he did not get a bite for quarter of an hour. The perch were accommodating in the main, and did not disappoint him, for at twelve o'clock — as he judged it to be by the height of the tide — he had seven dozen in the boat, and they were still biting as greedily as when he first commenced. He had two lines on board, and he tried the experiment of using them both at the same time, though without much success ; for perch are fastidious, and require a great deal of attention. While he was pulling in a fish upon one line, the sly rogues in the brine stole his bait from the other, and he came to the conclusion it was not best to have too many irons in the fire at once.

Paul did not like to abandon the field while it was yielding such a rich harvest; but he was a prudent fisherman, and not disposed to run any risks. The tide would turn in less than two hours, and he knew it would be impossible to run up to Bayville against both wind and tide. The old boat was not equal to any such emergency, and he reluctantly wound up his line and made sail for home.

The seven dozen perch were to be cleaned, and when he got fairly under way he missed John, for it was difficult for him to skin fish and work the boat at the same time. Seating himself in the stern, he passed his arm round the tiller, — for there was no comb to keep it in place, — and commenced his labors. He soon found that he was working at a great disadvantage, and he exerted his ingenuity to devise a plan for overcoming the difficulty. Taking a small line, he made the middle of it

fast to the end of the tiller; then passing it round
the cleets, he tied the ends together. This apparatus
kept the tiller in its place, and he could change
it to any required position by pulling the line.
Resuming his labors upon the fish, he found his
plan worked very well, and the perch were in
readiness for market when he reached the shore.
After securing the boat, he hastened with the
fish to the cottage, where his dinner was waiting
for him. His mother congratulated him upon his
success, and told him that Captain Littleton had
been to see her during his absence, and that she
was entirely reconciled to his new occupation.

The most difficult part of the business, in Paul's
estimation, was yet to come — that of selling the
fish. As he left the house with his precious load
of merchandise, he could not help feeling that the
grand scheme was still an experiment, for it had
not been demonstrated that Bayville would buy six
or eight dozen of perch every day. It was a large
place, containing about six thousand inhabitants;
and as he walked along, he brought his mathemat-

ical knowledge into use in an attempt to convince himself that the market was large enough to keep him busy during the season. At the least calculation there were six hundred families in the town, and probably a thousand. If each family would buy a mess of perch once in ten days, it would make six hundred dozen in that time, or sixty dozen a day; but, to make allowance for over-estimates, he was willing to reduce the total one half, and call it thirty dozen a day. The fisherman would supply a large portion of the demand, but he concluded that he should have no difficulty in selling all the perch he could catch.

Passing the house of Captain Littleton, the next was that of Major Nettle, and he resolved to make his first attempt to sell. The gentleman was not at home, and the servants didn't know any thing about it; and he was just leaving when Thomas Nettle accosted him.

" What have you got, Paul ? "

" Perch ; do your folks want to buy any ? "

" Yes, I guess they do. Where did you catch them ? "

" Down at Rock Island; I am going down every day."

" Are you, though? I should like to go with you some time."

" I shall be glad to have you. I have gone into this business."

" What for? "

" Since my father died, I have to do something to help my mother," replied Paul, not caring to announce to his friend the whole of his stupendous plan.

" Do you expect to do any thing at this business? "

" Certainly I do; I made two dollars at it yesterday."

" Did you though? "

" Do your folks want any perch to-day? "

" I guess they do; how much a dozen? "

" Seventeen cents," replied Paul, who had decided to be moderate in his prices.

" I will speak to my mother."

Thomas returned in a short time, and took two

dozen of the fish, and paid the money for them.
Overjoyed at this success, he proceeded to the
next house; but though he was eloquent in regard
to the freshness and fineness of his wares, he could
not make a trade. He met with no better success
at the next three or four places at which he called,
and he began to feel a little discouraged. But the
next house in his way was a large, genteel boarding house, and he had the satisfaction of selling
four dozen at the price he had before fixed, though
he had almost made up his mind to let them go
at ninepence. The gentleman who kept the house
was pleased to get the perch, and wanted the
young fisherman to bring him some three times
a week for the present, for his boarders were very
fond of them.

Paul could scarcely contain himself for the joy
he felt, as he glanced at the only remaining dozen
of his stock, and at the very next house he disposed of them. With a dollar and nineteen cents
in his pocket, he walked towards home, proud as
a lord of his success. The result of this day's

9 *

work afforded him far more satisfaction than that of the preceding day, though the proceeds were considerably less; for he was conscious of the influence of Captain Littleton's generosity in the transaction. But the second day's triumph was achieved by his own unaided labor and skill. What he had done this day was a fair specimen of what he might hope to do in the future.

"Sold out so soon, Paul?" said his mother, as he entered the kitchen.

"Yes; I had good luck. They took four dozen at the boarding house. I think if I had had twenty dozen I could have sold them all. There is a great deal of difference between perch just out of the water, fresh and good, and perch which have been dragged about in a fish cart, under a hot sun, for two or three days."

Mrs. Duncan fully agreed with this sage remark, and did not think it improved any kind of fish to keep them a great while after they were caught.

"One dollar and nineteen cents, mother; here

is the money," continued Paul, emptying the contents of the wallet into her lap. "What do you think of the fishing business *now*, mother?"

"It has proved to be a very good business so far; but you must not expect people to eat perch all the year round, Paul. They will get sick of them after a while."

"Then I shall go farther off; but there are other fish besides perch, and I don't intend to confine my operations to one kind. There are eels, and smelts, and cod, and haddock; and if worse comes to worse, I can go into the clam trade."

"What a boy!" laughed Mrs. Duncan. "You are so determined that I have no doubt you will succeed."

"If I don't, it shall not be my fault," replied Paul, complacently.

"But you don't mean to follow this business all your life?"

"Why not?"

"The life of a fisherman is not the pleasantest in the world."

"That's according to one's taste. If I only had a good boat, I can't think of any thing that would suit me better."

"It is hard work."

"So much the better. You said that five dollars a week would support the family. Now, if you have no objection, I will save up all I make over that sum, till I get enough to buy a boat."

"Certainly, Paul; and if you give me three dollars a week, or even two, I can get along very well."

"I shall not do that, mother. I am going to support the family, any how; and I wish you wouldn't take any more bags to make."

"You mustn't think of doing too much, Paul."

"Too much! I shall be idle half the time, at this rate. Here I am, with my day's work done at three o'clock in the afternoon. I don't want you to do any thing, mother, but take care of the house, as you always used to do."

"There will certainly be no need of it, if you get along as well as you expect. How much will such a boat as you want cost, Paul?"

"Well, I don't know; when I buy I want to get a first-rate one."

"How much do you think?"

"Fifty to seventy-five dollars; but I won't think of such a thing yet a while. The old one will do very well for the present. I can save up something every week, and little by little, I shall make up enough to get just such a boat as I want."

"You might take the money from the life insurance; for Mr. Freeman will perhaps sell us the house, if we pay nine hundred dollars down."

"I won't do that, mother. My boat shall be bought with my own earnings."

"I will lend you the money, then."

"No, I won't get in debt."

"But a new boat would be safer."

"The old one is safe enough; all the fault I find with her is, that it takes her so long to get down to the fishing ground."

Paul resolutely refused to run in debt, or to touch the money which had been appropriated for

the purchase of the house. He intended, when he
had time, to fix up the old boat, and rig a jib on,
which he thought would overcome his principal
objection to her.

When he went to bed that night, he entered
the proceeds of this day's work in his book, and
then, with pardonable pride, he congratulated himself on the sum total of the earnings of the two
days.

CHAPTER VIII.

PAUL TAKES A COLD BATH.

THE limits of our little volume do not permit us to follow Paul Duncan into the minutiæ of his prosperous business, and we are reminded that great events in his experience are yet to be introduced. He was successful in his undertaking, though, like all in this inconstant world, he was subjected to trials and disappointments. There were some days when it was so rough off the rocks that he could not fish; and there were others when he had to travel many miles before he could sell his fish. During John's vacation, his receipts amounted to about two dollars a day, which went a great way in counterbalancing the ill luck of the next week. On an average, he earned about a dollar a day.

He had won a reputation in Bayville which helped him a great deal in disposing of his mer-

chandise. People saw him working hard to supply the place of his father, and they were glad to
encourage him, as there are always found enough
who are willing to help those that help themselves. The sympathy and kindness of his neighbors were a great assistance to him, and no doubt
without them his fish would have oftener been a
drug in the market.

Paul inherited some portion of his father's me-
chanical skill; and on the first stormy day after he
set up in business, he commenced his contem-
plated improvements upon the old boat. She was
a very poor subject to work upon, but he got out
the wood for building a half deck over her, which
he fitted on as he had opportunity. A short bowsprit was added to her rig, and his mother made
him a jib, which he cut out himself. Thus refitted, the old boat, though her main defects could
not be remedied, was much improved, and worked
better than before. She was far from coming up
to the young fisherman's ideal of a trim craft, and
he cherished a strong hope that before many years

had passed away, he should have the satisfaction of sailing such a boat as his fancy had already clearly defined. The time was closer at hand than he suspected.

One day, early in the month of July, Paul was making his way home from the rocks in a smart blow. While he was fishing, the wind had hauled round to the north-east, and continued to freshen till it became a reefing breeze. He had got but a small fare of fish, for the heavy sea had interfered with his operations. He disliked to leave the fishing ground, but it was sufficiently evident to him that a storm was approaching. He had often promised his mother that he would be very careful, and the present seemed a proper time to exercise that caution. John was with him, and in spite of this bold youth's most earnest protest, he got up the anchor and made sail for home.

" What are you afraid of, Paul?" demanded John, with evident disgust.

" You are a pretty sailor! Don't you see it is going to blow a young hurricane?"

10

"What if it does? I should like to be out in a blow once. I want to know what it's like," replied the reckless boy.

"You may know now, before you get home. Don't you see the white caps on the waves off to windward?"

"I like the looks of them, and it's fun to skip over them."

"I don't want to worry mother. She's at the window by this time, looking out for the boat. Do you think there is any fun in making her uneasy? Besides, I don't think it is safe to stay here any longer. There comes the Flyaway under jib and mainsail."

"What of it?"

"She went down to be gone all day. What do you suppose she's coming back for at this early hour?"

"I suppose Captain Littleton didn't want to make the women seasick," promptly replied John.

"Would the foresail make them sick? She has taken the bonnet off her jib too. Captain

Littleton knows when to expect a gale, and we shall have it soon."

So it seemed by the working of the little boat, for she tossed up and down on the waves like a feather, and thrust her bows under so far, that John had to waste some of his enthusiasm upon the baling kettle. Paul had not hoisted the jib, for the mainsail was all the old craft could stagger under, and her youthful skipper expected soon to be obliged to reef. The Flyaway was at the eastward of the island, driving over and through the waves like a phantom. The spray. was dashing over her bows, and her jib was wet several feet above the boltrope. She was working to windward till she could clear the island, when she would have the wind free into Bayville Harbor. Perhaps some of my non-nautical young readers will need to be informed that working to windward means sailing in a zigzag line in the direction from which the wind blows.

The Flyaway ran close in to Rock Island, and tacked at the very spot where Paul had just been lying at anchor, and his boat was not more than the eighth of a mile distant from her. The boys could distinctly see the ladies and gentlemen on board of her, and replied to signals of recognition that were made to them. There were several children on her deck, and Paul identified Carrie Littleton in a little girl of ten, who was waving her handkerchief to him. As the yacht came up into the wind, and before the boom swung over, the young lady jumped upon the taffrail to obtain a better view of them. To the horror of all who saw the accident, the heavy spar struck her on the shoulder, and she was knocked overboard. The Flyaway, catching the wind, flew from the spot, and when the little girl rose to the surface of the water, she was out of the reach of those on board of her.

"Heavens and earth!" shouted Paul, jumping up from his seat, as he beheld the catastrophe. "There is Carrie Littleton knocked overboard by the boom!"

"O, dear! She will be drowned!" gasped John.

"Take the helm, John! Don't blubber! Quick!" cried Paul, as he leaped forward, and brailed up the sail. "Now, hard down! Lively!"

The boat, which was making very good head-way, came, about, and was headed towards the island. Shaking out the sail again, she bore down towards the unfortunate girl. In the mean time, the Flyaway had luffed' up; though she was nearer to Carrie than Paul's boat, she was rapidly drift-ing to leeward. Her tender, which was a light canoe, had been placed upon deck, and the crew were launching her; but as they did so, by the clumsiness of some one engaged in the operation, she filled as she struck the water, and they were obliged to haul her up again with the halliards.

Before they had made fast to the painter of the canoe, Paul had reached the scene of the disas-ter; but poor Carrie had sunk beneath the angry waves. She had evidently been injured by the blow of the boom, and was unable to make any exertion.

"Now mind your eye, John!" snouted Paul,

10 *

as he dashed off his coat and shoes. "When I dive, throw her up into the wind."

"Look out, Paul; don't do that," remonstrated his brother. "You will be drowned yourself. Fish her up with the boathook. Mother will——"

The intrepid youth, disregarding the terror of his brother, dived over the bow of the boat the moment he saw the form of the poor girl, which was revealed to him by the white dress she wore. John obeyed the instructions he had received, but before Paul reappeared, with the drowning child in his arms, the boat had drifted some distance from the spot.

"Haul aft your sheet!" gasped Paul, when he had regained breath enough to speak.

John obeyed, but his terror had almost paralyzed his arm, and his action was not so prompt as it might have been; but the boat slowly gathered headway, and moved towards the struggling youth. Paul battled manfully with the big waves, which repeatedly swept him under, and determined to die rather than drop his helpless burden.

As the boat came down upon him, Paul supported Carrie with one arm, and grasped the gunwale with the other.

"Luff up!" said he. "Now, catch hold of her, and help haul her in," he added, as the boat came up into the wind.

John did his best, but he was not strong enough to draw the lifeless form into the boat. Bidding him hold on for his life, Paul leaped into the boat, and drew her in.

"Keep her away for the yacht," cried Paul, as he placed the form of the poor girl — for he was not certain that it was still animated by the vital spark — in the bottom of the boat.

Turning her face down, in order to let the water run out of her mouth, he used all the efforts his knowledge and his means would permit to promote her restoration. In a few moments the boat came alongside the Flyaway, though John, in the excitement of the moment, stove her gunwale in, and had nearly added another calamity to the chapter of accidents.

Captain Littleton jumped into the boat as she struck the side, and seizing the beloved child in his arms, leaped back upon deck, and then rushed into the cabin.

"Hand up your painter, Paul, and come on board, both of you," said Captain Gordon, the skipper of the Flyaway.

"Ay, ay, sir," replied Paul, too much interested in the fate of poor Carrie to think of parting company with the yacht.

The fishing boat was made fast at the stern of the Flyaway, and she stood off again to clear the rocks around the island. All the party on board had followed Captain Littleton into the cabin, to learn the condition of his child, or to render assistance in restoring her. It was very fortunate that Dr. Lawrence was one of the company, for he was a very skilful man, and under his direction the measures for the relief of Carrie were conducted.

The Flyaway had reached her berth at the mouth of the river before the efforts for the

child's restoration promised to be effectual. It
was found that the blow of the boom had not
seriously injured her. In an hour after the yacht
reached her moorings, she was able to speak, and
the doctor ordered her to be taken home.

Before the yacht reached her berth, a pair of
anxious eyes, from the chamber window of the
cottage, had discovered the dingy old boat towing
at her stern. The mother's heart almost failed
her, as her imagination pictured some dreadful
calamity that had happened to her boys. Filled
with dreadful forebodings, she seized her shawl
and bonnet, and hastened to the landing, in the
rear of Captain Littleton's house. They were
bringing home the boat in which her boys had
gone out, and she feared that one or both of them
had been lost. She tried to believe that the yacht
had overtaken them, and that Captain Littleton
had invited them on board; but her fears were
stronger than her hopes.

When she reached the landing place, she saw
that the gunwale of the old boat was stove, and

her heart sank within her. There were several persons at the landing, and she told them what she feared. One of them took a skiff and rowed out to the yacht. Paul and John were both in the cabin, and when the messenger came alongside, the captain called them on deck. Seeing Mrs. Duncan on the shore, they got into their boat, and soon joined her.

"I never was so glad to see you before in my life!" exclaimed the delighted mother, clasping them both to her bosom. "Why, Paul, you are as wet as a drowned rat! You have been overboard; I know you have!"

"That's so, mother; but I didn't upset nor fall overboard. I went over of my own free will."

"Yes, he did, mother," interrupted John. "Carrie Littleton was knocked overboard by the boom, the Flyaway's boat got swamped, and she drifted to leeward, and we came about, and bore down on her, and Paul dived after her, and I worked the boat, and we hauled her in, and took her on board the Flyaway — didn't we, Paul?" and John sputtered as though his own mouth had been full of salt water.

"We did," replied Paul.

"You will catch your death a-cold, Paul. Do come home now."

"I must take the boat round."

One of the bystanders, all of whom had listened with eager interest to the particulars of the accident, volunteered to perform this service for him; and Paul, shivering with cold, ran home, followed by his mother and John.

"Where is Paul Duncan?" demanded Captain Littleton, after the doctor had ordered his daughter to be carried ashore.

"Gone, half an hour ago, sir," replied Captain Gordon.

"God bless him!" fervently ejaculated the grateful father; and he proceeded to give directions for the removal of Carrie.

CHAPTER IX.

PAUL BECOMES SKIPPER OF THE FAWN.

THE heroic act of Paul, in saving the life of Carrie Littleton, was the principal topic of conversation in Bayville for the next week. Of course it was the unanimous vote of the people that Paul was a hero, and there was some talk of giving him a complimentary dinner, and making speeches at him; but the good sense of the strong-minded men and women of the place prevailed, and he was not treated with the honors that turn the head of a third-rate politician. But every body thought something ought to be done, and after a full week had passed by, every body wondered that Captain Littleton did not do something; that he did not make Paul a present of a gold medal, or give him a check for a hundred dollars. The gossips could not find out that he had done any thing more than thank Paul, with tears of gratitude in his eyes, for the noble service he had rendered him. The captain had the reputation of being a very liberal man, but the glory of his good name seemed to be rapidly passing away.

Paul attended to his business as usual, and seemed to give but little heed to the compliments that were showered upon him. When any one spoke to him about his gallant deed, he tried to turn it off, declared he had only done his duty, as sentimental heroes generally do, and he did not think he had done any very great thing, after all. But notwithstanding all this seeming indifference, Paul was proud of the act that had made him famous. He was conscious that he had done a noble deed; and his own heart assured him he deserved the praise which was so liberally bestowed upon him.

Above all, he was grateful for the opportunity of serving Captain Littleton, who had been so kind to him and to his mother. He was happy

11

in the thought of having saved that darling child
from a watery grave, and he had given the fond
father a good reason for being his friend as long
as he lived. Paul never thought of any reward;
he hoped Captain Littleton would not give him
any thing, for that would deprive him of one half
the satisfaction the act had afforded him.

Another week passed by, and still, to the astonishment and disgust of the gossips of Bayville,
Captain Littleton took no further notice of Paul's
heroic deed. Mrs. Green, who was Mrs. Duncan's
nearest neighbor, ventured to suggest that the captain was a mean man, and she wouldn't have
thought it of him.

"What would you have him do?" asked Paul,
to whom Captain Littleton's reputation was as dear
as that of his mother, or even of his dead father.

"What would I have him do?" repeated the
old lady. "Why, he ought to give you a hundred dollar bill, all for your own. At least he
ought to give you fifty."

"I don't want any thing, Mrs. Green," said Paul,
stoutly.

"That's nothing to do with it. He could just offer it — couldn't he? He is a rich man, and a hundred dollars is no more to him than a hundred cents to me. It is downright mean, there."

"I don't think so, marm. Captain Littleton has done every thing he could for mother and for me, and I'm sure I was glad to have a chance to do something for him."

"That may be; but it don't look well for a rich man like him to let you save his little daughter from drowning, and then only say thank'ee for it."

"I think it does, Mrs. Green, and I hope he will let the matter rest just where it is."

"There is no danger now but what he will. If he ever meant to do any thing for you, he would have done it before now."

"I am perfectly contented, marm, and I only wish the neighbors were as easy about it as I am."

"It ain't none of the neighbors' business, I know," added Mrs. Green, a little tartly; "but I can't look on and see such meanness without speaking of it. It don't make no difference who I say

it to, neither; I had just as lief say it to Captain
Littleton, as say it to you and your mother. That
is just what I think, and I may just as well speak
it as think it."

It was a remarkable fact, under the circumstances, that Mrs. Green never did give Captain
Littleton the benefit of her opinion on this subject.
Perhaps she wronged him by her silence, thus de-
nying him the practical advantage of her criticism
for the direction of his future life. But Paul
never liked Mrs. Green so well after this, for she
had spoken ill of him whom he honored and es-
teemed.

Our young fisherman, apparently unmoved by
the honors that clustered around his name, pursued
his humble avocation with pride and pleasure —
with pride, because he had been successful by his
own unaided exertions; with pleasure, because he
was actually relieving his mother from the entire
burden of supporting the family. Since the rescue
of Carrie, perch, tom-cod, flounders, and tautog
had been in greater demand than ever, for many

of the rich people bought fish, even when they did not want them, just for the sake of patronizing the young hero; and the poor people ate fish oftener than they would if their admiration for the little fish merchant had been less.

The long summer vacation had commenced, and the boys were let loose from school for six weeks. John felt as though he had been emancipated from a dreadful drudgery. He could scarcely repress his exuberant joy, as he carried home his books on the last day of the term. Paul reproved him for his dislike of school, and told him he might see the day when he would appreciate the advantages of a good education.

" I don't dislike school," growled John, though it was a good-natured growl.

" Yes you do; you hate school," added Paul. " If you did not, you would not be so glad to get away from it."

" 'Not that I love Cæsar less, but I love Rome more,' " replied John, laughing.

" What do you mean by that?" demanded Paul,

11*

amused at the attitude into which his brother threw himself as he uttered the quotation.

"Not that I love school less, but I love fishing more; that's the idea," replied John.

"I hope you will get enough of it in six weeks, then."

"I hope so, but I don't believe I shall. At any rate, I'm going every day, and I'm going to be first mate of the Blowout."

"The what?"

"The Blowout; that's what I have christened the old boat."

"That's a very beautiful name."

"And she's a very beautiful boat," laughed John. "I wish you had a better one."

"So do I; perhaps I may have, one of these days."

"Somebody's got a new one, Paul," added John. "There is one moored off Mercantile Point. Did you see her?"

"No; whose is she?"

"I don't know; I saw her come up the bay

as I came home from school. She's a perfect beauty."

"We will go over and see her by and by," said Paul, for a new boat was an object of interest to him, and he always improved the opportunity to inspect any strange craft that visited the bay. "But, John, we must be off early on Monday morning, and the jib of the Blowout, as you call her, wants mending. We will go down and sew it up."

The brothers repaired to the beach, where the old boat was now high and dry upon the sand, and taking a little box containing the thread, needles, and wax for mending the sail, they commenced their labors. Their busy hands soon completed the task, and the Blowout was otherwise prepared for duty on Monday, for Paul never went near the boat on Sunday. They were now ready to visit the new craft; but when they had pushed their boat down into the water, Paul saw a gentleman enter the cottage of his mother.

It was Captain Littleton; and Paul delayed their departure, thinking that he might want to see him.   Presently his friend appeared on the bluff.

"Are you busy, Paul?" he shouted.

"No, sir; I will be with you in a moment."

"Stay where you are;" and Captain Littleton descended the steep path which led to the beach. "You were going out — were you?"

"We were, sir; but it is of no consequence," replied Paul. "John says there is a new boat over by the Point, and we were about going to see her."

"Very well, I will go with you;" and Captain Littleton stepped into the boat.

"Our boat is not a very nice one for you to sail in," apologized Paul.

"I have been in worse ones than this, Paul; and I have seen the time when I would have given all I had in the world for even so dingy a boat as this."

"When was that, sir?" asked John, very promptly; for he stood his ground, unawed by the dignity of the richest man in Bayville.

"Get your boat under way, and I will tell you about it," replied Captain Littleton.

Paul shook out the mainsail, and then pushed off the boat, while John hoisted the jib. The former then took his place at the helm, and the latter seated himself amidships, both eager to hear the story of the captain. It was fortunate for them that the old Blowout was a very heavy sailer; otherwise they could not have obtained the whole of the story, which was long and very interesting and exciting. We have not space to repeat the story, but it was all about a shipwreck, and clinging to a broken spar for forty-eight hours, without food or water, and being rescued when life was nearly gone.

"So you see, Paul, I should have been very comfortable even in a worse boat than yours," added the story-teller, as he completed his narrative.

"I should like to be shipwrecked once," said John, musing.

"Should you, my fine fellow?" exclaimed the captain.

"I should, sir, just to see how it would seem."

"It would seem very uncomfortable, my boy; and I recommend you never to express such a .wish again. Many shore people think there is something very fine and romantic about the sea, or even about a wreck; but half a day's experience would teach them better. For my part, I was very glad when I escaped the necessity of going to sea, even as master of a vessel."

"There is the new boat," interrupted Paul, as the Blowout rounded Dog Island, which had before concealed the new craft from their sight.

"Isn't she a *ripper!*" exclaimed John.

"Don't use such words, John," added Paul, in a low tone.

"She's a very fine boat," said John.

"She has a broad beam, but she looks as though she would sail well;" Paul continued.

"Keep her away a little; we will go on board of her if you like," said Captain Littleton.

Paul, though he would not have ventured on board of the new craft if he had been alone, ran the Blowout alongside of her, for he was satisfied that the presence of his friend would free him from the charge of trespass. John made fast the painter to the new boat, and the party leaped on board.

"Isn't she a beauty!" ejaculated John.

"A perfect beauty," added Paul, with enthusiasm. "She will sail like a bird."

"You see she has air chambers at the bow and stern," said Captain Littleton. "You cannot sink her."

The boys examined her from stem to stern, and their eyes sparkled with pleasure, as they rested upon her useful and elegant appurtenances. John looked over her gracefully rounded stern, and found there the words, FAWN — BAYVILLE, in raised gilt letters; and he immediately gave utterance to his opinion that the Fawn of Bayville couldn't be beaten.

"How do you like her, Paul?" quietly asked Captain Littleton.

"First rate, sir; she is the finest boat I ever saw."

"Do you think she would sail well?"

"I know she would."

"Suppose we try her. You may hoist the fore and main sails."

"Does she belong to you, sir?"

"She belongs to a friend of mine; but we will try her."

Paul and John hoisted the sails, and got every thing in readiness to slip the moorings, when the captain wished John to take the Blowout over to her berth, and they would take him on board again. He consented, and the two boats were soon headed towards the beach; but the Fawn made three rods as often as the Blowout made one.

At last John worked the clumsy old boat up to the beach, and jumped on board the Fawn. The language with which he expressed his satisfaction at her performance under sail was not very elegant or well chosen; but it undoubtedly expressed his opinion, so that no mistakes in regard to his meaning could have been excused.

"You like her, do you, Paul?" asked Captain Littleton for the tenth time.

"Very much indeed. She is a beauty! Who owns her, sir?"

"She belongs to a young friend of mine — one Paul Duncan."

"Sir! What!"

"Exactly so, Paul. She belongs to you, and henceforth you are to be the skipper of the Fawn."

12

CHAPTER X.

PAUL AND JOHN ARE VERY MUCH EXCITED.

PAUL was overwhelmed with astonishment and delight at this unexpected declaration. His eyes filled with tears, and he could not utter a word to express the gratitude that filled his heart.

"Yes, Paul, you shall hereafter be the skipper of the Fawn," repeated Captain Littleton.

"And I shall be first mate!" exclaimed John, jumping up and clapping his hands with rapture.

"Yes, and you shall be first mate, John; for I have not forgotten that a part of my debt of gratitude for the rescue of my daughter is in your favor, my fine fellow. The Fawn shall be owned between you."

"Thank you, sir," replied John; "but it was Paul that saved Carrie."

"If you had not handled the old boat well, Paul

could not have saved her. You are fairly en-
titled to a share of the honor of that noble ex-
ploit."

"But, Captain Littleton," interposed Paul, "I
do not want to be paid for what I did. It was
only my duty to save Carrie."

"Every body does not do his duty in such a
trying time as that was, Paul. But I have not
said a word about paying you."

"I know you have not, sir; but I suppose that
is what you mean."

"I mean nothing of the kind, my boy. I could
not pay you. There lies the Flyaway," continued
the Captain, pointing to his beautiful yacht; "she
cost me six thousand dollars. If I were called
upon to decide which I would lose, Carrie or the
Flyaway, which should I choose?"

"The Flyaway, of course."

"Then the Flyaway would have been but a
small compensation for my child. Nay, if I were
called upon to decide between my child and all I
am worth in the world, I would sacrifice all my

earthly possessions for her. Then, if I paid you all I could pay you, it would be all I have, Paul. You will not, therefore, consider this boat as a reward for saving Carrie's life."

"I didn't mean that, sir," stammered Paul, "but —— "

"But you thought I meant it. I did not. I shall never be able to discharge the debt of gratitude I owe you."

"We will call it square, if you please, sir," said John.

"We will not, my fine fellow," added the Captain, laughing at John's matter-of-fact speech. "I had been thinking of making you a present of a boat before this event happened, Paul; but I confess, the gift was hastened by your daring act. The long and the short of the whole matter is, that we will consider the Fawn a memorial of the rescue of Carrie, and not a reward. She is a strong, well-built, and safe boat, and I think will just answer your purpose. By the way, how do you like her name?"

" First rate, sir."

" I think I heard you suggest that name for a boat, once."

" It is just the name I should have given her," replied Paul, so excited by the extraordinary event of the hour, that he could hardly keep his seat.

" I am glad, then, that she suits you in every re-spect. Now, if you will put me ashore near my house, I will leave the Fawn and her owners to their future destiny."

Paul landed Captain Littleton on the pier be-hind his house, and after pouring out his thanks for the magnificent gift, they parted company. The Fawn was headed away from the rocks, and again stood out into the bay before the fresh breeze.

"I say, Paul, isn't this a stunner?" exclaimed John, suddenly jumping up from his seat, after he had remained silent and motionless for the full space of five minutes — a most extraordinary oc-currence with him.

" What do you mean by a ' stunner,' John," asked Paul, with dignity.

12 *

" Well, what a — what a — what a thundering thing this is!" sputtered John. "Only to think —— ".

" I wish you wouldn't use those slang phrases. You let them out before Captain Littleton, just as though he were one of the fellows."

" He's one of 'em, any how. He's a trump!"

" Will you quit using slang words?"

" I'll try."

It must not be supposed that Paul was always so particular in regard to the choice of words; but at the present time, the idea of being owner of such a craft as the Fawn, and being the friend of such a man as Captain Littleton, inspired him with a dignity he did not always possess.

" Talk like a gentleman, if you can, now there is some prospect of your becoming one," continued Paul.

" I will try; but I want to talk about the boat now. Isn't she a — a beauty! I should like to try her with the Snow-Bird."

" Very likely we may have a chance. She's too

good to go a fishing with," said Paul, glancing around him at the cushioned seats in the standing room.

"It won't hurt her any; we can take the cushions out when we fish."

"We must use her for that, I suppose. But Jack Starr lets his boat, which is not half as good as this, for four dollars a day. Perhaps we can do a little business of this kind."

"Very likely we can; folks always want to go down in the best boat."

"We can suit them, then. Where are you going now, Paul?"

"I am going to run in, and let mother see her."

"Good! Won't her eyes stick out?"

"She will be surprised," replied Paul, in tones of gentle rebuke.

The Fawn was run carefully upon the beach, and John was despatched for his mother. While he is absent, we will improve the opportunity to give our young readers a better idea of the new boat than they have yet obtained. She was about eighteen feet long, and very broad for her length. Her bow was very sharp, and her build combined the advantages of being a safe boat and a fast sailer. She was schooner-rigged, carrying a jib, foresail, and mainsail; and there was a staysail in the cuddy for use when the wind was light.

The deck of the Fawn extended over about half her length, and under it was a cuddy, or small cabin, containing two berths, both of which were furnished with proper bedding. There were four lockers, or closets, accessible from the standing room, where the boys could keep their fish lines, knives, spare ropes, and other articles required on board.

The Fawn was rather large for a boy of Paul's age to handle, but as this fault would be corrected in a year or two, Captain Littleton thought it would be well to prepare for the future as well as the present. But the rigging was so arranged that the new boat was hardly more difficult to manage than the old one, and she was capable of saving at least one half the time which the Blowout occupied in going to and returning from the fishing ground.

While John was absent, Paul again examined every part of the Fawn. He looked into all the lockers, sounded the copper air-chambers, lay down upon each of the berths, and hoisted the mainsail, just to see how easily it could be done. The examination was satisfactory in every respect.

"Mother, mother!" shouted John, as he rushed breathless into the house, where Mrs. Duncan was getting tea; "come down to the beach just as quick as ever you can."

"What is the matter, John? What has happened?" asked Mrs. Duncan, alarmed by his earnest manner.

"Come down quick, mother; don't stop a minute!"

"What has happened?"

"Nothing, mother; only come."

"Is any thing the matter with Paul?" she inquired, as she hastily grasped her sun-bonnet, and followed John out of the house.

The enthusiastic youth did not wait for the more tardy steps of age, but tumbled recklessly down the steep path, and leaped into the boat.

"Where is mother?" demanded Paul.

"She is coming. I wish we had a cannon; we would fire a salute."

"No use of burning powder for nothing. There she comes."

But it was some time before Mrs. Duncan could reach the beach, and John occupied the interim in various antics, such as running up the shrouds of the Fawn, hoisting and lowering the jib, lying down on the bobstay, and finally in tumbling overboard while attempting to perch himself on the end of the bowsprit. This accident did not in the least disturb his equanimity, and he had just shaken himself, like a Newfoundland dog, when his mother reached the beach.

"Whose boat is that, Paul?" asked Mrs. Duncan, who, during the last moments of her walk, had been gazing with admiration upon the trim craft.

"Mine, mother," replied Paul, with assumed indifference.

"Mine, too," added John.

"We own her together," said Paul

"Own her together? What do you mean by that? Haven't you learned better than to make sport of your mother, boys?"

"It is ours, certain true, mother!" cried John.

"You don't mean so?"

"It is a fact, mother," replied Paul.

"Why, where, what in the world —— "

"That's it, mother; I knew you'd come to it," interposed John. "To make a long story short, Captain Littleton made us a present of her."

"Dear me!" .

"Isn't she a beauty?"

"I should think she was."

"Come, mother, we are going to take you out to sail in her. You shall try her right off," said John. "Jump aboard."

"But I can't jump aboard. The water is knee-deep around her. Besides, supper is almost ready."

"Never mind the supper. Jump in."

"I can't jump in. Where *have* you been, John? You are as wet as a drowned rat!"

"I fell into the tub just now; but never mind that."

"But I do mind it; and you must go up and have on dry clothes before you go any where."

"We will go up and have supper, and after that we will take you out," said Paul.

John was disposed to rebel at this step; but Paul was firm and decided, and made fast the Fawn to the stake in the beach. When they reached the house, the young rogue, sorely against his will, was compelled to retire to his chamber and change his clothes. Even then, dripping as he was from the effects of his cold bath, when Paul went up to call him to supper, he found him standing at the window, in his wet garments, gazing with intense interest upon the Fawn, as she lay moored at the beach.

Paul, notwithstanding the flutter of emotions in his bosom, ate his supper with dignity and pro-

priety, and several times admonished his brother
that he behaved more like a young monkey than
a reasonable human being. Yet Paul was excited,
and so was his mother. The former talked of the
good times he should have down the bay, and
the latter speaking of the forethought of Captain
Littleton in having the copper air chambers placed
in the boat. She was glad the Fawn was a life
boat, and she could feel a great deal easier, now,
when her boys were away on the water.

Supper was finished, and John, in his impatience to get on board the boat again, conde-
scended to wipe the dishes, while Paul cleared
off the table. Matters thus expedited, the party
were ready to embark, and repaired to the beach
for that purpose. John was absolutely frantic in
his efforts to perform his duty as first officer of
the Fawn, and in his eagerness had nearly
drowned his mother, and swamped the boat. If
the halliards of the new craft had not been new
and strong, he would certainly have broken them
in hoisting the sails. Paul was disgusted at his

13

conduct, and it wás only when he threatened to put him on shore that the mate subsided into the appearance of a tolerable calm.

The party had a very pleasant sail; but Johı almost cried with vexation, after the boat was properly secured at her moorings, to think he could not go on board of her again till Monday morning. Paul was scarcely less excited than his brother; but the consciousness of being the head of the family restrained any outbreak of enthusiasm on his part. His thoughts ran deeper and extended farther into the future.

As he retired that night, he examined the columns of his account book, and had every reason to be satisfied with his success. His excitement had moderated, and he looked upon the Fawn as a new blessing, and in his heart thanked God, from whom all his blessings came.

He regarded his fortune as already made, for, little by little, he felt sure of achieving it.

CHAPTER XI.

PAUL'S FIRST CRUISE IN THE FAWN.

AT breakfast time the next morning, John Duncan was among the missing. His mother had charged him, when he first got up, to study his Sunday school lesson, which, in the extraordinary excitement of the preceding evening, had been neglected. Paul searched for him in their chamber, and in all the other apartments of the house; but he was not to be found.

Neither Paul nor his mother had any fears that he had run away or committed suicide; so that his absence produced more of indignation than alarm.

"He must have gone down to the boat," suggested Mrs. Duncan.

"If he has, I will throw him overboard."

"O, no, my son! you would not do that."

"He has no business on board the boat on Sunday."

"That is very true, Paul; but I suppose he cannot keep his thoughts away from her. I don't much wonder, either."

"I don't know as I am very much surprised myself," added Paul, whose second thought was more reasonable than the first.

When he considered how many times his thoughts had wandered to the beautiful Fawn, and how many times he had permitted himself to anticipate the pleasure of the first cruise in her, during the morning, he was more charitable towards his younger brother, who had only done what he had thought.

"I will find him," said Paul, taking his cap.

"Don't be harsh with him, Paul, for he means right, only he has not so much strength of mind as you have."

"I won't be hard upon him."

"Because you are older than he is."

"I won't be a hypocrite, mother, and I may as

well own that, while getting my lesson, I could not help thinking of the new boat. I don't want you to believe I am better than I am."

"It is very natural that you should think of her; but you must try not to do so. It is almost a pity the boat had not come on Monday, so that you could have had a whole week to think about her before Sunday."

Paul ran down to the beach, and discovered that the door of the cuddy of the Fawn was open. Jumping on board, he found John stretched out upon one of the beds, apparently very busily engaged in studying his Sunday school lesson.

"What are you doing here, John?" demanded Paul, though his tones were very gentle.

"I am getting my lesson," replied John, as demurely as though he had not chosen an unusual place for the exercise.

"Have you got it?"

"All but two questions."

"What made you come here?"

"I couldn't help thinking of the boat, and I

13 *

made up my mind that I could get my lesson here better than any where else."

"I'm afraid you haven't studied it much."

"Hear me say it, then," said John, jumping up, and handing Paul the book.

"Not now; breakfast is ready. But I want to have an understanding with you, as you are part owner of the Fawn, that neither of us go on board of her on Sunday, unless there is some strong reason for it. Will you agree to it?"

"I shan't want to after to-day."

"No matter; will you agree to it?"

"Yes; but there was a strong reason this morning."

"What was it?"

"Why, I wanted to see her."

"That's no reason at all. I have just as hard work as you have to keep away from her; but we mustn't do every thing we want to do. Come, lock the cuddy, and let us go up to the house."

"That's honest, and not a bit like preaching," said John to himself, as he locked the cuddy, and followed his brother up the hill.

"I am trying to make money, John, but I don't believe money is all we have to live for."

"Of course not; there is a good deal of fun to be had in this world, that costs money instead of bringing it in," answered John, very soberly; and it was evident that his thoughts were not upon his Sunday school lesson.

"I wasn't speaking of fun. Up to the time I went to sleep last night I was thinking how I should make money; this morning, the first words I saw when I opened the Testament to get my Sunday school lesson, were, 'For what is a man profited, if he shall gain the whole world, and lose his own soul?'"

"I guess you had the nightmare last night, and have got the blues this morning," said John, trying to get up a laugh, in which, however, he did not succeed very well, for it is hard, even for a tolerably well-disposed boy, to make fun of serious things.

"I mean just what I say, John; you needn't laugh. I feel that we have something else to live for besides money. It is a very pleasant thing to make money ——"

"Little by little," added John, adopting his brother's favorite motto.

"But I wouldn't be a rich man, if I had to be as mean and selfish as old — no matter who. He is poorer than I am now, with his hundreds of thousands. I mean to lay up good principles ——"

"Little by little," interpolated John.

"Little by little, if you please; but even a little every day will make a good man one of these days. A good thought every day will make a man rich in good principles; at any rate, my book says so."

"How can a fellow help thinking of the boat, if it is Sunday?"

"We must try to think of our lesson, and when we go to church, of what the minister says. I am going to try and not think of the Fawn again till I wake up to-morrow morning."

"I am willing to try, but it's no use. I wish Sunday was over, and Monday had come."

How many boys and girls have thought the same thing! That Sunday, whose moments seemed so heavy, was a golden opportunity which may have passed never to be recalled. We are indebted to the still hours of the quiet Sabbath, to the leisure moments of our daily life, nay, to the sleepless couch of pain and suffering, and to the bitter time of woe and bereavement, for some of the best and truest thoughts which illuminate our mortal pilgrimage, and which give birth to our good resolutions. A single instant may produce an impression upon the heart which shall last to the end of life.

The words of the Scripture which Paul had read and heard read a hundred times, without feeling the tremendous truth they contain, were now full of meaning. They seemed to connect themselves with his individual future, and to have produced an impression which the excitement of possessing the new boat could not overcome. He was in the right frame of mind to receive such an impression, and it had an important influence on all his subsequent career.

As the family seated themselves at the breakfast table, Mrs. Duncan improved the opportunity to enlarge upon the duties we owe to ourselves and to others, in connection with the Sabbath day. It is true that John's levity occasionally detracted from the effect of the lesson; but it was not wholly lost, even upon that wayward youth.

Paul struggled hard with his thoughts during the day, and he was surprised, when night came, to find how successful he had been. It had been a good day to him, and he had profited by the instruction it afforded him; for the first step towards moral or spiritual improvement is to fasten the mind earnestly upon some moral or religious topic.

Long before the sun rose the next morning, Paul and John were on the beach. And when Mrs. Duncan rang the bell out the window for them to come to breakfast, they had dug a bucket of clams, and had prepared the Fawn for her first trip down the bay.

"You won't be anxious about us now, mother,

for we have a boat that can't sink," said Paul, as he took the luncheon prepared for them.

"I shall feel easier now."

"Besides, you know we have two good berths on board the boat, and we should be just as comfortable, if out all night, as though we were in our own beds up stairs."

"That may be, but I hope you will never stay out all night, when you can help it."

"We shall not, mother; you may depend upon it; but we might get aground; or the wind might die out, and the Fawn is too large to be rowed up."

"I shan't worry about you, if I can help it, for I know you are very careful, Paul."

The boys hastened down to the boat, and Mrs. Duncan went out upon the bluff to see them off. The wind blew fresh from the south-west when they started, and the Fawn went out under jib and mainsail only; but even with this sail, she flew like a racehorse over the waters.

"Shall I hoist the foresail, Paul?" asked John.

"I think not; she is doing very well."

"But she will do better with the foresail."

"Let well enough alone."

"I want to see her do her best."

"I have promised mother a hundred times that I would be careful; and if she should see us put on all sail in this wind, though there might not be any danger, she would think we were going straight to the bottom. We will not hoist the foresail."

This answer satisfied the impatient boy, and in a short time they reached the perch ground; but either there were no fish there, or they had not got the hang of the new boat; for the fishermen could hardly get a bite. After trying for an hour, and catching only half a dozen small perch, the boys became disgusted with their ill luck, and it required but little persuasion on the part of John to induce Paul to get up the anchor, and go farther down the bay.

An hour's sail brought them to a reef of rocks, which was quite a noted locality with the fishermen. The Fawn was anchored in a safe place, and the young fishermen threw over their lines. Better success attended their efforts here, and in three hours they had caught eight dozen fine perch, besides ten handsome rock-cod.

While they were fishing under the lee of the rocks, they had scarcely noticed that the wind had been steadily increasing, and that it was producing a heavy sea in the bay.

"We shall have a chance to find out what kind of a sea boat the Fawn is," said Paul, as he weighed the anchor.

"I am glad of it," replied John.

"The wind is freshening every moment," said Paul, casting an anxious glance to windward.

"Hope it will blow a gale."

"I think we shall get more than we want."

"Not more than I want, at any rate."

Paul hoisted the jib, and the Fawn rushed out among the white-capped waves; but she walked over them so majestically, that John declared she could weather any gale that ever blew. For a time she breasted the foam of the head sea in a

14

most gallant manner; but the wind came in fearful gusts, increasing in violence every moment, till Paul came to the conclusion that it was no longer safe to carry the jib and mainsail, and proposed to set a reefed foresail. John scouted the idea, but he did not want the mainmast blown out of her, and consented to the change.

.John took the helm, and Paul, after lowering the jib and mainsail, hoisted the reefed foresail. The boat rode easier then; but as the wind and tide were both against them, it was soon discovered that she made no headway. As the gale steadily increased in fury, Paul would not attempt to carry any more sail, though John insisted that she could bear the jib and a close-reefed mainsail.

It was evident to Paul that, unless he put on more sail, he could not beat up to Bayville against the tide; but it was clearly imprudent to carry any more sail, and for two hours more the Fawn struggled with her hopeless task without making a single mile.

"What are you going to do, Paul?" asked John, impatient, but not terrified by their situation.

"We can't beat up in this sea."

"I know that."

"We will run over to Farm Island, and anchor under the lee of the high bluff;" and he headed the Fawn in the direction indicated.

CHAPTER XII.

PAUL SLEEPS ON HIS WATCH.

FARM ISLAND was about two miles distant, and as the Fawn had the wind on the quarter, it required but a short time for her to reach her haven of safety. Under the high bluff on the seaward side of the island, the water was comparatively tranquil; and here Paul anchored.

"We are all right now," said he, with a feeling of relief, as he took in the foresail.

"When do you suppose we shall get home?" asked John.

"I don't know; we will not borrow any trouble, so long as we are in a place of safety."

"Mother won't think we are in a place of safety," added John.

"Yes she will; I have often told her that, when a gale came on, I should always get into a safe place, and keep quiet till it was prudent to run home."

" It is lucky we are in the Fawn instead of the Blowout."

" We should not have gone down so far in the old boat. I felt so safe in this craft that I did not mind much about the weather."

" We have been safe enough all the time; and if you would only have put on the jib and reefed mainsail, we should have been at home by this time."

" I did not think it was prudent to do so. I may have been mistaken; if I was, I have erred on the safe side."

"I suppose we must sleep on board," said John.

" If you don't like the idea, you can go on shore, and sleep at the farm house."

" But I do like the idea; we have good beds, and I had just as lief sleep here as in my own bed at home. In fact, I am rather glad we are caught."

" I thought so," said Paul, laughing; " but there is one thing we are not prepared for."

14 *

" What is that ? "

" Supper."

" I wish we had a frying pan and a furnace ; we could have some fried perch for supper."

" As we have not those things, we must make the best of what we have. Our luncheon is all gone ; but there are two or three crackers in the locker, which I threw in from the old boat."

" We shan't starve before morning," replied John, whose philosophy was proof against an empty stomach.

" I know that ; but it would be a good deal better to have some supper, if we could get it."

" Can't we go on shore ? "

" No, we can't land on this shallow beach. It wouldn't be safe to get aground here."

Both boys were very hungry, for it was now nearly night, and they had taken their lunch in the middle of the day. The crackers were eaten, and washed down with a drink of cold water from the jug ; but it was a dry and unsatisfactory supper, and Paul resolved in future to keep the

Fawn provisioned for such an emergency as the present.

The wind still blew with undiminished violence, and the black clouds indicated rain. By and by the darkness came on, and there was no longer any prospect of getting home before the next day. Just before dark, a man hailed them from the shore, and offered them a bed at the farm house; but Paul thanked him and declined the offer, at the same time hinting that they had nothing on board to eat.

"Come ashore, then, and get some supper," replied the man.

"We can't get ashore; we draw too much water," answered Paul.

"I will bring you off then."

The man pushed a skiff into the water, and soon came alongside the Fawn.

"You have got a fine boat here," said he.

"Yes, sir; she is a very nice boat."

"But this is pretty heavy weather for boys to be out. Whose boat is she?"

"She belongs to us."

"To you?" replied the man, apparently much astonished.

"Yes, sir; she was given to us by Captain Littleton."

"O, ho! so you are Paul Duncan."

"Yes, sir."

"And I understand why he gave it to you. Come, boys, you must go up to my house and stay with me to-night. I should rather have Paul Duncan under my roof than the governor of the state."

"We must stay on board, sir, to look out for the boat. If any thing should happen to her in the night, I should never forgive myself for deserting her. We have a nice place to sleep," continued Paul, opening the doors of the cuddy, and pointing to the two berths.

"That looks very comfortable, but there is not much fun in sleeping on board a small boat such a night as this will be. But come up to the house, and have some supper."

"Thank you, sir; we will do that, for we are

both very hungry. Stop a moment. John, hand out two or three of those rock-cod. Won't you take these, sir?"

"I am much obliged to you for them. Though we live so near the fish, we don't have much time to catch them," replied Mr. Drake, — for that was the name of the farmer, — as he threw the fish into his skiff.

The two boys got into the boat with him, and he rowed them on shore. They were warmly welcomed by Mrs. Drake and the children, and a nice supper was soon placed before them; but all the arguments and expostulations of the farmer and his wife could not induce them to spend the night at the house. Paul was too fearful in regard to the safety of the Fawn to leave her, and John was too deeply smitten with the romantic idea of sleeping on board, to think of spending the night in any other manner. Mr. Drake, therefore, reluctantly put them on board their boat again.

"Now, Paul, we are in for it," said John, as he saw the farmer land, and draw up his skiff upon

"Yes, and it is going to be a very dirty night. I think the wind has shifted since we went ashore," replied Paul.

"So do I; we feel it as much again as we did."

"It blows full as hard as it has any time to-day."

The boys sat down in the standing room, and had a long talk about home and mother, and wondered what she would think because they didn't come home. It was now quite dark, and there was not a single star to relieve the gloom of the scene. John even went so far as to admit that it "looked kind of pokerish," and he was glad they were in so comfortable a place.

"Come, Paul, isn't it time to turn in?" asked John, after they had come to the unanimous conclusion that it was a decidedly stormy night.

"You can turn in, John, if you want to," replied Paul.

"Ain't you going to sleep any to-night?"

"I have no idea of leaving the Fawn to take care of herself in such weather as this."

" Are you going to sit up all night?" asked John.

" It isn't customary, I believe, on board ship, for all hands to turn in, and let the vessel take her chance."

"There is no danger here."

" If we both go to sleep, we may wake up and find ourselves nowhere. Suppose the wind should change to the eastward; we should be fully exposed to all the fury of the storm."

" I didn't think of that. Suppose we watch by turns, then."

" Very well; I will keep the first watch, and you may turn in as soon as you please."

" What is that?" asked John as he heard three strokes of a bell.

" There is a large ship at anchor off there."

" But it isn't three o'clock yet. Her clocks must be out of order."

" Three bells; that is half past nine o'clock."

" I don't understand it; how should three bells mean half past nine?" inquired John, who did not like to leave any nautical subject till it had been fully investigated.

"It begins to rain, and we may as well sit in the cuddy;" and they both retreated to the little cabin, and seated themselves on their berths. "If we only had a lantern to hang up in here, we should be perfectly at home."

"We will bring one next time; but about the bells, Paul?"

"Well, they have two watches on board ship, which are called the larboard and the starboard watches. In large vessels, they are under the care of the first and second mates. The twenty-four hours, on board ship, are divided into five watches of four hours each, and two dog-watches of two hours each. During these watches, the bell is struck every half hour; that is, one bell at half past eight; two bells at nine, three bells at half past nine; and so on, till twelve, when it is eight bells, at which time one watch goes below, and the other comes on deck. At half past twelve the bell strikes one again; at one it strikes twice, and so on. Do you understand me?"

"I think I do; but when are the dog-watches?"

"From four to six, and from six to eight in the evening. They always strike the bells by twos, as you heard just now. But, John, it rains like fury."

"So it does, but it is a dry place in this cabin."

"I wish we had a lantern, for it is as dark as a pocket in here. It would make it so much pleasanter. But you must turn in now, or you will not be able to stand your watch."

"I think I will."

John took off his boots, and placed himself under the blanket and comforter of his berth, for there were no sheets. He gaped several times, and tried to continue the conversation with Paul; but the poor fellow, worn out with the fatigue and excitement of the day, was soon fast asleep. Paul listened to the sound of his heavy breathing, between the splashes of the waves as they broke upon the bow of the boat, till he began to feel sleepy himself, and then, wrapping the great-coat, which he always carried with him, closely around his

15

body, he went upon deck to see if there was any change in the weather or the position of the boat.

It was clear to him that the wind had been hauling round to the eastward, for the Fawn tumbled about as she had done out upon the open waters of the bay. As he lay down upon the deck to examine the cable, so as to assure himself that it was not chafing the boat, a huge wave broke over the bowsprit, and he would have been drenched to the skin, if his coat had not been water-proof.

The rain continued to pour down, and Paul retired to the cuddy again. It was a weary, lonely watch, and he was so tired he could hardly keep his eyes open. But it seemed to him that the violence of the gale was subsiding, and he again went upon deck to satisfy himself on this point. There was still a heavy sea, but he was satisfied that the wind had very sensibly abated. Six bells sounded from the ship as he returned to the cuddy.

Throwing himself on his berth, he listened for a while to John's sonorous snores, and before he was sensible of the danger of his position, he was sound asleep himself. Worn out by the labors of the day, he could no longer keep his eyes open.

He woke with a start, — for he was conscious that he had forsaken the post of duty, — and hastened upon deck. Eight bells from the ship told him it was midnight. The wind had nearly subsided, but it rained very hard, and the heavy sea continued to break over the bow of the Fawn.

John was still sleeping like a log, and Paul, though it was time for the larboard watch to be called, had not the heart to wake up his brother. As the gale had subsided, the boat seemed to be no longer in danger, and he decided to turn in and finish his nap. But while he slept, the wind, which had abated only to come with still greater violence from another quarter, steadily increased in fury, till it blew a gale from the north-east.

The pitching of the boat soon startled Paul from

his slumbers, and he rushed out into the standing room to find that the Fawn was rapidly dragging her anchor, and was in imminent peril of being dashed to pieces on the rocky shore.

CHAPTER XIII.

PAUL MAKES A NIGHT RUN IN THE STORM.

"JOHN, John!" shouted Paul, when he realized the dangerous situation of the Fawn.

But the first mate of the craft slept too soundly to be disturbed by mere words, and the skipper had to shake him before he came to his senses.

"What is the matter, Paul?" asked he, as soon as he could get his eyes open and realize where he was.

"Put on your great-coat and shoes, and come out here, and be lively about it," cried Paul.

John obeyed, and before he was ready to join Paul in the standing room, he began to apprehend the state of affairs on board, for the furious wind and the angry waves that stormed against the hull and rigging of the Fawn told their own story.

15 *

"What's the trouble?" he asked, as he joined his brother.

"Don't you see there is a gale of wind down upon us?" replied Paul, sharply.

"Well, what of it?" demanded the young salt, with provoking indifference.

"A good deal of it; the boat has dragged her anchor, and at this rate will be upon the rocks in fifteen minutes! Come, be alive, and don't stand there like a log."

"What shall I do? You are the skipper, and I am ready to do any thing you say," replied John, who was by this time fully awake.

"Can we pay out any more cable?"

But this was a useless question, for Paul knew very well that the cable was all out. Our young readers may not all understand the meaning of Paul's question. If the vessel rides at anchor with a short cable, her motion, as she rises and falls with the sea, raises up the shaft of the anchor, which has a tendency to detach the flukes, or points, from the bottom. But Paul had been careful the night before to give the Fawn all the cable he could spare; and it was evident, therefore, that the anchor was not heavy enough, or that there was no holding-ground at the bottom.

"There is only one thing we can do, John," said Paul, desperately, after he had fully examined the situation of the boat.

"Say on, then," replied John; "I am ready for any thing that you say."

"We must get up the anchor, and leave this place."

"Up it is, then."

"But this is an awful bad time, and an awful bad place to hoist a sail."

"Let her drive; we shall go it well enough. It blows like all-possessed; but what's the use of having a life boat, if you can't go out in her when it blows?"

"Stand by the fore halliards, then," cried Paul. "The sail is close-reefed, just as we used it yesterday."

The foresail was hoisted, and slammed with tremendous fury in the fresh gale. The boys then grasped the cable, and it required the full effort of their united strength to weigh the anchor; but the task was accomplished at last, and Paul leaped to his place at the helm. Laying her course parallel with the shore of the island, the Fawn dashed over the furious waves, within ten rods' distance from the breakers on the beach. In a few moments she passed beyond the reach of this peril, and rushed out among the billows of the open bay.

It was a fearful night even for strong men to venture upon the stormy sea; it was doubly perilous for these two boys; yet they had no choice, for to avoid a greater danger they had chosen the less. But the Fawn behaved in a very gallant manner, and her noble bearing promised to achieve all that could be done for the safety of the young fishermen. Notwithstanding the violence of the gale, she rested buoyantly on the top of the waves, and did not seem to labor in her course.

"Do you know where you are, Paul?" asked

his brother, after they had sat in silence for half an hour.

"Certainly I do; there is South Point light dead ahead."

"Yes; but there is any quantity of rocks between us and the light."

"I know that; but I know where they are just as well as I know where the kitchen is, when I get into the house. Don't talk to me now, John; go below, and turn in, if you like."

"Don't you want me?"

"No."

Paul did not think that John could act upon this suggestion, in such a storm and in the midst of so many perils; but he did, and as the young skipper heard no more from him, he concluded he was asleep.

"What a fellow!" thought Paul. "He could sleep in the midst of an earthquake or a tornado. Well, let him sleep; he is tired enough."

The Fawn dashed madly on, yet under perfect control, and the gallant skipper, when he saw, through the deep darkness, the white breakers on Rock Island, felt entirely relieved from the responsibility which had before almost crushed his spirits, for it was plain sailing after he had passed that point and the dangerous reefs which environed it. If the Fawn could stand such a sea as that, she could stand any thing, and her character was fully established for the future.

His spirits rose as he neared South Point light, which was not more than a mile and a half from his mother's house. He whistled merrily, to give expression to his satisfaction, as he passed the light, for he and the boat were now safe beyond a peradventure. Taking an extra turn in the foresheet, he laid the course of the boat a little closer to the wind, which soon brought her into the comparatively still water behind Long Island.

He saw the cottage of his mother now, and a light was burning in her chamber. He was grieved to see this, for he feared she might be sick, or that in her anxiety for the safety of her boys, she had sat up all night thinking of them. But in a few moments, he let go the anchor off the beach, and lowered the foresail. After making every thing secure on board, he hauled the old boat, which he had moored there in the morning, alongside. John was still asleep; neither the paying out of the cable, nor the noise of Paul's feet, as he furled the foresail, had roused him from his deep slumbers, and the skipper decided to let him finish his night's rest on board.

Sculling the old boat ashore, he ran up the hill, and knocked at the side door of the cottage.

"Who's there?" asked his mother.

"Paul."

The door was opened, and the fond mother clasped her son to her heart, while the great tears coursed down her furrowed cheeks.

"I am so glad you have got back!" exclaimed she; "I was sure you were drowned. Where is John? He isn't with you, Paul! O, he is —— "

"Fast asleep on board the Fawn, mother."

"Then he is safe."

"Yes; safe — yes."

" You have had a terrible time of it — haven't you ? "

" Not very bad, mother; the wind and tide were against us, and we couldn't get up without carrying more sail than I thought it was safe to carry; so I ran under the lee of an island, and anchored."

" But what did you start back in the night for ? "

" The wind hauled round to the north-east, and blew so that we dragged our anchor, and had to make sail to keep off the rocks."

" And John is safe, you say ? "

" Perfectly safe.   But why are you not in bed, mother ? "

" I couldn't sleep in such a tempest as this, when I knew my boys were on the water."

" Well, go to bed now, then, for I must go on board again and clean my fish."

" You shall do nothing of the kind!   I will warrant you haven't had a wink of sleep all night long."

" Yes; I slept two or three hours."

"Go right up stairs, and go to bed, then. You will kill yourself, working all night, and losing your sleep."

"But John is asleep in the cabin of the Fawn. Shall I leave him there? Suppose the boat should go adrift?"

"Well, then, go down to the boat, and go to bed there. You needn't clean your fish yet."

Paul decided to adopt this suggestion, and in a few moments he was snoring with his brother in the little cabin of the boat.

It was six o'clock when the first officer of the Fawn began to show signs of life, and it was fully quarter past six before he realized, in the fullest sense, that he was still in the land of the living. An unpleasant dream that the gallant craft had been dashed in pieces on Rock Island reef, and that he, the before mentioned first officer of the schooner Fawn, had been thrown upon the rocks, where an enormous green lobster, about the size of a full-grown elephant, had seized him in one of his huge claws, and borne him down among the rock weed

16

and devil's aprons for his breakfast, happily proved
to be a mere fantasy of his slumbering faculties. .

John sat upon his berth and congratulated himself upon his escape from the claw of the lobster.
Then the occurrences of the night, the run off the
lee shore, and the white capped billows that had
growled so in the gloom, began to come to his
recollection, and he realized that they had had a
tough time of it. But it was all right now, for
though the rain pattered upon the deck above him,
the boat did not pitch much. And there was Paul
fast asleep in the other berth; of course it was
all right, or he would not be there.

"But where are we?" thought John. "That's
the next question. The last thing I remember was,
that we were driving like mad over the rough sea.
Then Paul told me to turn in; and I did, but I
could hardly keep in my berth, the boat rolled and
pitched so. Of course Paul couldn't get up while
the wind blew so, and he must have anchored
under some island. I wonder where we are."

At last John came to the conclusion that he

could find out by simply walking out of the cuddy into the standing room. Acting upon this brilliant idea, he soon ascertained that the Fawn was at anchor near the beach of Bayville. He was somewhat astonished at the fact, and then paid a very high, though inaudible, compliment to the sleeping accommodations of the Fawn, whereof he was first mate.

He then returned to the cuddy, — he and Paul invariably dignified the little place as the *cabin*, — and found that Paul still slumbered. He was considerate enough not to wake him, for he knew that he had had a hard time of it; but it occurred to him that their mother might be desirous of knowing whether they were still in the land of the living or not, and he decided to go up to the house and reveal that important fact. It was very affectionate of him to think of his mother, after he had been snoring like a trooper all night; but John, in spite of his waywardness, was a kind-hearted boy, and he came to the unanimous conclusion — he and John — that it was not right to let his mother worry any longer about them. She would be astonished to see him alone, and would immediately make up her mind that Paul was drowned; and he should have the pleasure of informing her that his brother still lived, and was fast asleep in the cabin of the Fawn, whereof he was captain, and he, the speaker, was first mate.

John, on his arrival at the house, walked into the kitchen where Mrs. Duncan was getting breakfast; walked in as he who does the ghost in Hamlet walks in — with the confident assurance that he is about to create a sensation.

" Well, John, you have got back. Did you sleep well, my son ? "

" First rate," growled John. " Why the deuce isn't she astonished ? " thought he. " She ought to be astonished to see me come home after being on the briny deep all night."

" You had a hard time of it — didn't you John ? "

" Well, rather hard; I slept like a log all night — except about half an hour. You didn't expect to see us back — did you ? "

"I was a good deal worried till Paul came up and told me you were safe, and that you were asleep in the cabin."

"O, ho! so Paul has been home—has he? That accounts for it. Paul is asleep in the cabin now."

"Let him sleep — he needs rest," replied Mrs. Duncan; and it was after nine o'clock when the family breakfasted that morning.

16 *

CHAPTER XIV.

PAUL SCOLDS THE FIRST OFFICER OF THE FAWN.

AFTER breakfast the young fishermen cleaned their perch and cod, and before dinner had disposed of the lot. From the proceeds of the sale, Paul purchased a small lantern, which was suspended in the cabin of the Fawn, for the darkness of that gloomy night was not soon to be forgotten.

The next day was clear and pleasant, and the boat went down as usual, and for more than a fortnight, no event worthy of a place in the history of Paul's fortunes occurred. The new boat worked admirably in every respect, and the boys were as proud of her as England has ever been of the Great Eastern. During these two weeks Paul had taken down three fishing parties, and had given them so good satisfaction, that his services in this line promised to be in demand. As he received four dollars a day for her, including the wages of himself and the first officer, he always welcomed such jobs, and John liked the fun of it even better than fishing, especially when there were any ladies in the party, for it was very amusing to him to see them in the agonies of sea sickness. He took a malicious delight in stowing them away in the berths in the cabin; yet in spite of the fun he made of them, John would do all he could to assist them.

Just before the arrival of the Fawn in the waters of Bayville harbor, Paul had been unanimously elected a member of the Tenean Boat Club. He was very grateful for the honor conferred upon him, but his business was such that he could not often pull an oar in the boat. The members of the club all treated him with a great deal of consideration, though they were all the sons of rich men; and Paul felt that, if he was not their equal in worldly possessions, he could hold his head up with the best of them in the management of a boat.

One day, when the young fisherman called at

the house of Major Nettle to sell fish, he met
Thomas in the garden, who unfolded to him a
magnificent project in which the Teneans — as the
members of the Boat Club were generally called —
were about to engage.

"We think of going on a cruise in the Flyaway," said Thomas.

"Where?"

"I don't know where yet; but we mean to be
gone a week or ten days."

"Who is going with you?"

"Captain Littleton, I suppose, though I had
just as lief he would stay at home."

"Of course he wouldn't let a lot of boys go off
for a week in the yacht, without some one to take
care of them," said Paul, with a smile.

"We can take care of ourselves; we don't want
any one to take care of us."

"How many of you are going?"

"Ten or twelve; we want you with us."

"But I can't go."

"Yes you can; why not?"

"I have to attend to my business."

"You can afford to take a vacation of a week or two, I should think."

Paul shook his head. He was delighted with the idea, and would have been very glad to go, but he could not think of neglecting his business to go away upon a pleasure excursion.

"You must go, Paul; the fellows all want you to go, and we shall have a first-rate time."

"I have no doubt you will; and I should be very glad to go with you if I could; but it is of no use for me to think of such a thing."

"It is not fully decided that we are to go yet; but Captain Littleton and my father have consented to let us have the Flyaway. We shall know all about it next week."

Paul continued his walk, but the project of the excursion in the Flyaway haunted his imagination, and it required a great deal of self-denial for him to forego the anticipated pleasure. He felt that the summer season was the harvest time of his business, and he could not afford to waste a week or two in idle play. "Little by Little," was his motto, and he was not willing that any of those "littles" should slip through his fingers.

When they went down in the Fawn the next day, he told John about the excursion, and that he had been invited to form one of the party.

"But I can't afford to go," he added.

"Why not? It won't cost you any thing."

"I shall lose my time, for the Fawn will lie idle at her moorings while I am gone."

"No, she won't. I will go a fishing in her every day."

"I think not, John."

"Do you think I can't manage her?" demanded the first officer, indignant that such an aspersion should be cast upon his nautical skill.

"She's too heavy a boat for you to manage alone."

"I will get a couple of fellows to help me; they will be glad enough of the chance."

"I dare say they will; but you are not quite old enough yet to run the boat yourself."

"What odds does it make how old I am, if I only know how to handle her? Could you work her any better if you were a hundred years old?"

"But you are reckless, careless, John; you know you are."

"I don't think I am; but I will promise to be very careful. You may take the foresail off, if you please, before you go; then you will be sure I shall not carry too much sail."

"I don't intend to go; so it is of no use to talk about it."

"You are a fool if you don't; that's all I have to say."

"You have a right to your own opinion, John."

"I wish I had a chance to go. I would give all my old shoes, if I could only be one of the party. What a glorious time they will have!"

Paul was of precisely the same opinion, but the idea of letting John run the Fawn during his absence was not for a moment to be tolerated. He would certainly run her on the rocks, or carry sail till the wind took the masts out of her.

As it was a very pleasant day, Paul decided to run down below, and try his luck among the cod and haddock; and they went farther out than they had ever been before. A fine lot of fish, including a mammoth cod, that had required the strength of both of them to pull out of the water, rewarded their enterprise.

The wind was very light, and instead of getting home before the tide turned, as Paul had calculated, they were two miles below Rock Island, when the ebb tide set in against them. To add to this misfortune, the wind entirely died out, and they were forced to come to anchor, to prevent drifting down with the tide. With a good wind they were only two hours' sail from home; but, as it was, there was a prospect of spending another night in the cabin of the Fawn — not a very unpleasant alternative, John thought, especially as they had a lantern, and plenty of provisions on board.

The cod and haddock had all been dressed, and there was nothing for the boys to do; so Paul went into the cabin and stretched himself on his berth. He had placed two or three books on board for such an emergency as the present, and he was soon absorbed in the contents of one of them. He did not read long, for a hard day's work is not a good preparation for literary labors. The book fell from his hand, and to the music of the flapping sails he dropped asleep.

It is a noticeable fact that fishermen can sleep twenty-four hours on a stretch. Many years ago, we went down a-fishing in one of the pinkey-stern schooners, which were much more common then in the waters of Massachusetts Bay than at the present time. The crew consisted of the skipper and three men, the former of whom was an old, weather-beaten fisherman, who had roughed it on the coast from his boyhood. We went down one night, intending to fish the next day, and return by sunset; but unfortunately a heavy rain kept us at our anchorage off Spectacle Island for twenty-four hours. The old skipper got out of his berth and ate his breakfast about ten, and after going half way

17

up the companion ladder, to smell the weather, turned in again, and slept till four, when he was called to partake of a greasy chowder. As soon as he had disposed of a reasonable allowance for four hearty men, he tumbled into his berth once more, and was not visible again till the next morning. The rest of the crew slept about two thirds of the time. They were the sleepiest men we ever encountered during their leisure; but even the old skipper suddenly joined the "wide-awakes" when we reached the fishing grounds.

Paul had already contracted this fisherman's habit, and while the Fawn lay at anchor, he slept like a rock. After amusing himself for an hour on deck, John went below to take an observation, and to announce the prospect of "a breeze from the southward," for he had discovered a gentle ripple on the water at a distance. But when he saw that Paul was "having his watch below," he quickly returned to the standing room, closing the cabin doors behind him.

"There is a capfull of wind," said he to himself, " and I will just show the skipper of the Fawn that I can handle her as well as he can."

He waited till the breeze reached her, and then, with as little noise as possible, he weighed the anchor, and took his place at the helm.

"All right, Captain Duncan; you can finish your snooze at your leisure," muttered he, congratulating himself upon the fact that he had got off without waking Paul.

The wind freshened into a nice little breeze, and the Fawn, close-hauled, rippled merrily through the water. Still Paul slept on, unconscious of the progress she was making, while John was jubilant over the success of his trick. He was obliged to tack so as to go to the windward of Rock Island, but he twice accomplished this manœuvre without disturbing the sleeper.

The boat was now up with Rock Island, and John, who could never see why Paul always wanted to keep half a mile away from this dangerous reef, laid her course very near the rocks.

"All right, my boy," said John, who had a

bad habit of talking to himself when there was no one present to whom he could address his remarks; "won't Captain Duncan be astonished when he comes out of the cabin!"

And Captain Duncan was astonished when he came out, for just as the rash first officer arrived to the conclusion that the boat had run clear of all the dangers of the navigation in that quarter, —

Bump! went the Fawn on a hidden ledge.

"What are you about?" cried Paul, angrily, as he rushed out of the cabin.

"About got aground, I should say," replied John, a good deal more astonished than he had calculated Paul would be.

"Let go your sheets! Take the boat-hook, and let us push her off, if we can," cried Paul.

Both the boys went to work, and after a few moments of hard labor, succeeded in pushing the Fawn off the ledge upon which she had struck.

"I suppose this is a specimen of your management," said Paul, as he hauled the sheets home, and seated himself at the helm.

"Rather bad management, I am willing to own," replied John, who felt that his reputation as a skilful navigator had departed in the twinkling of an eye.

"Next time, when you undertake to sail the Fawn without me, don't you do it. You would be a pretty fellow to run the boat if I were away a week; there wouldn't be a board left on her ribs in three days."

"It hasn't hurt her any, Paul."

"I suppose it hasn't; but it would have been just the same if it had been blowing a ten-knot breeze."

But John felt that, if it hadn't hurt the Fawn any, it had hurt himself a great deal; and he made a tremendous great resolution to be more careful in future. The boat reached her mooring in good season, notwithstanding the detention.

17 *

CHAPTER XV.

PAUL GOES ON A CRUISE IN THE FLYAWAY.

"There has been a gentleman here to see you," said Mrs. Duncan, when Paul went to the house.

"Who was he?"

"He left his name and residence on a piece of paper, and wants you to call and see him this evening," replied Mrs. Duncan, handing him the address of the gentleman.

"Charles Morrison, Chestnut Street, third house from the depot," said Paul, reading the paper. "What does he want?"

"He said something about hiring your boat next week."

"What, the Fawn?"

"I suppose so; but he wants to see you, at any rate."

"Does he want me to go with her?"

"I'm sure I don't know."

After supper Paul went to see Mr. Morrison, and found that he wanted the Fawn for the whole of the following week, and that he did not want a skipper. He was góing down to Bleakport to spend a week, and he wanted a good boat, which he could not procure at the place. He offered to pay fifteen dollars for the use of her, and to restore her in as good condition as when he took her.

This was certainly a good offer, and Paul concluded that he could not do better; but he was not prepared to give a decided answer, and promised to see the gentleman again the next evening.

On his return home he found Henry Littleton and Thomas Nettle waiting for him. The arrangements in regard to the excursion in the Flyaway had been completed, and the two boys had come to urge Paul to join them.

"When do you sail?" asked Paul.

"Next Friday."

"And how long shall you be gone?"

"About eight or ten days," replied Henry Littleton. "My father is going with us."

"I have got a good offer for the use of my boat next week," answered Paul, musing, "and I don't know but I will go."

"That's right, Paul; we must have you with us, at all events."

"Father says we ought to have you with us," said Henry.

"I will talk with my mother about it, and if she is willing, I think I will go."

"We have talked with your mother already, and she is perfectly willing you should go."

"I will let you know to-morrow."

The boys left him, saying he must certainly go with them, and Paul went into the house to talk over the matter with his mother.

"Do you think I can go, mother?"

"To be sure you can go," interposed John. "What is the use of talking about it?"

"I did'nt ask you, John," said Paul, with a smile.

"I don't see why you can't go," replied Mrs. Duncan. "I suppose there is no more danger of your getting drowned than there would be if you staid at home."

"He will certainly be drowned, mother," added John.

"We shall be safe enough."

"Then you had better go."

"I have got a chance to let the Fawn for fifteen dollars; and that would be about as much as I should make if I staid."

"And if you let her, I shall go skipper. Shan't I?" demanded John.

"I think not; Mr. Morrison will be his own skipper."

"Then I won't agree to it. I am part owner of the Fawn," said the first mate, pouting like a school girl.

"You agreed to let me manage the Fawn at the beginning," added Paul. "You can't do any thing with her alone, except run her on the rocks."

"I don't want you to manage me out of her in

that manner," growled John. "I have as good a right in her as you have, and I don't mean to stay on shore here a whole week, sucking my fingers, when there is fun to be had."

While they were discussing this important question, which even threatened a rupture in the partnership between the young fishermen, Captain Littleton was admitted by Mrs. Duncan.

"What's the matter, boys? You are not quarrelling, I hope," said Captain Littleton, as he entered the room, for he had heard a portion of one of John's excited speeches while at the door.

"O, no, sir," replied Paul. "I have got a chance to let the Fawn for a week, and John is opposed to my doing so."

"Is he? I am sorry for that. Mr. Morrison spoke to me about a boat for the week, and I recommended him to you. I had a motive for doing so, for I want you to join the excursion in the Flyaway. I thought you would like to go, if you could do so without any loss."

"Thank you, sir. I should like to go very

much; and when I got this chance to let the Fawn, I about made up my mind to go."

" Then it is all right; but I am sorry John will not consent to the arrangement."

" I don't want to stay on shore a whole week," pouted the first mate of the Fawn. " If they would only take me as skipper, I should like it first rate. What shall I do with myself for a whole week on shore ? "

" I don't see as I can go, then," added Paul.

" Well, I don't want to keep you from going, Paul ; " and a better feeling seemed to be roused in John's bosom.

" I can't afford to let the Fawn lie idle for a week, in the busy season," continued Paul.

" Can't I go a-fishing in her while you are gone ? "

" Certainly not; you can't have my share to smash up on the rocks," said Paul, a little tartly. " You know you ran the boat on the rocks this very afternoon."

John felt a little lame here, and he did not

venture a reply. He had sacrificed his reputation as a navigator by carelessly attempting to run too near the reef, and he felt that his brother's conclusions were correct.

"Well, at any rate, I won't keep you from going in the Flyaway, whatever I do. I will agree to let her to Mr. Morrison."

"That's generous, John. You have got the right kind of a heart beneath your jacket, though you have an odd way of showing it sometimes," said Captain Littleton.

"John means right, sir," added Paul.

"I like to have a little fun myself, as well as the rest of the fellows," continued John, "but I am willing to stay at home for Paul's sake."

"That's the right feeling, my boy," replied Captain Littleton; "and if your mother is willing, you may go in the Flyaway."

"Hoo-ray!" shouted John, jumping out of his chair, and performing some gymnastic feats, that astonished the visitor and the family. "I may go — mayn't I, mother?"

"I have no objection, if Captain Littleton thinks it is safe."

"He will be as safe as my own son, Mrs. Duncan," added the captain.

"Hoo-ray!" shouted John again.

"Come, my son, behave yourself, or they won't want such an unmannerly fellow in the company."

"I will be as polite as a French dancing master."

John was in luck again, and for the following three days he talked of nothing but the cruise of the Flyaway. Even sailing in the Fawn seemed tame to the idea of going off one or two hundred miles, and visiting towns and cities he had never seen, and had never before expected to see. He could hardly sleep nights, and when he did sleep, it was only to dream of being out of sight of land, or of occupying a berth in the cabin of the yacht.

Paul concluded his bargain with Mr. Morrison, and made all his preparations for an absence of a week or ten days — a longer time than he had ever been away from home before. He cleaned up the Fawn for Mr. Morrison, and split wood

18

enough to last his mother a fortnight. It had
already been decided that the yacht should go to
the eastward, and visit Gloucester, the Isles of
Shoals, Portsmouth, and Portland; and to be prepared for the excursion, he carefully studied all
the maps and books he could procure, which gave
any information in regard to these places.

The Flyaway was to sail on Friday at high
water. For more than a fortnight, Captain Gordon had been training the boys of the Tencan
Club to serve as "able seamen" on board the
yacht. There were twelve of them, including
Paul, who were to join the party. More than
half of them were sixteen or seventeen years old;
so that they were strong enough to do all the
work required in the management of the vessel.
They were all well trained, and every one of
them knew his duty on board.

Besides Captain Gordon, who was to command
the yacht, there was Captain Briskett, who had
for many years been the master of a coasting
vessel, and knew every rock and shoal between

Boston and Eastport. Dick, the colored steward, was to retain his place during the cruise. Captain Littleton was to go as a passenger. John Duncan was nominally appointed cabin boy.

Friday came, and the officers and crew of the Flyaway were all on board. The anchor had been hove short, and the mainsail hoisted; the hour for sailing had arrived, and she only waited the coming of Captain Littleton. He had gone to Boston that morning, and his return was momentarily expected.

When the amateur crew had grown very impatient at his non-arrival, he appeared; but only to inform them that he had just received a telegraphic despatch from New York, which would compel him to start for that city in the afternoon.

"Now, boys, what is to be done?" asked he. "Will you postpone the trip for a week?"

"I suppose we must," replied Henry; but the faces of the whole crew were wofully elongated.

"I must give it up altogether, then," added Paul, bitterly disappointed; and John was ready to howl at the idea of not going.

"I will see what can be done," continued Captain Littleton, as he called Captain Gordon aside.

For a few moments they were engaged in earnest conversation together, and the boys waited with anxious interest for the result of the conference.

"Captain Gordon thinks he can take care of you, and I have concluded to let you go without me."

"Hurrah!" shouted several of the boys.

"But, boys, I must put you on honor to behave well during the cruise. Will you do it?"

"We will." ·

"And obey the orders of Captain Gordon in all things, whether you are on board or on shore?"

"We will," replied all the boys at once.

"Very well; I shall trust you. If I return soon enough to join you at Portsmouth, I shall do so. Good by, now, and a pleasant cruise to you;" and Captain Littleton went over the side.

"Good by, sir," replied the crew.

"That's first rate — isn't it?" whispered Tom

Nettle, as the captain departed. "I am glad he isn't going."

"So am I," replied Frank Thompson.

"We shall not have him watching us all the time. Let me tell you, there is fun ahead now," added Thomas.

Captain Briskett, who was to be first officer of the Flyaway, as well as pilot, summoned them to the windlass to heave up the anchor; and in a few minutes the yacht was standing down the harbor under all sail. The Tencans gave three rousing cheers, and then distributed themselves in various parts of the deck to enjoy the exciting scene.

"All hands aft," said Captain Gordon, when the yacht had reached the open bay.

"Ay, ay, sir," replied several, as the crew took their places in the standing room.

"Now, boys, we must make our arrangements. When a ship goes to sea, it is customary to divide the crew into two watches. I shall take the starboard watch, and Captain Briskett the lar-

18 *

board.   Each of us will choose a man in his turn
till all are taken."

"Go on," said Captain Briskett.

"Henry Littleton," replied the skipper.

"Paul Duncan," added the pilot.

And so they proceeded till all the boys were
chosen, except John, who resented the slight thus
put upon him.   To satisfy him, therefore, he was
taken into the captain's watch.

"There are only eight berths in the cabin,
boys, and you must draw lots for them," continued the master; "but they are all wide enough
to hold two each.   Now, if you want to pair off,
you can do so."

Lots were drawn, and Paul and Henry were to
occupy the same berth.   Again John found himself thrown out of the calculation; but the captain
said he would make a bed for him on a locker,
and he was satisfied.   The boys then went below
to see their berths, which had all been numbered
for the occasion.

CHAPTER XVI.

PAUL WITNESSES A MUTINY.

WHEN the Flyaway had passed Farm Island, and reached the fishing ground, she lay to, for the purpose of enabling the crew to catch a few cod and haddock, for the chowder and fry. But cod and haddock are singularly obstinate at times, and persistently refuse to appreciate the angler's endeavors in their behalf. They were so on the present occasion, and it was two hours before the chief of the culinary department could say there were enough to satisfy the ravenous appetites of the sixteen persons on board. Some of the boys had actually decided that fishing was a nuisance, but they were just as fond of chowder as those who enjoyed the fun even of catching only one fish per hour.

As fast as they were caught, Dick dressed them

añd prepared them for the chowder pot or the frying pan. There were some queer fish caught, including quite a number of sculpins, "a wolfer eel,"—so Captain Briskett called him,—and a large catfish. The latter was an ugly monster, having dangerous-looking teeth, with which he laid hold of every thing that came in his way. There was also in the collection a large scate, or ray, which called forth some rather large fish stories from the two experienced skippers on board.

As the culinary department was now supplied, the yacht stood away for Gloucester, which was to be her first port. They had a fine wind, and before the chowder was ready, the Flyaway was in sight of the Reef of Norman's Woe.

"Dinner is ready," said Dick, at last, for the stomachs of the boys had been in a state of rebellion for two hours.

There was a grand rush for the cabin; but, to the astonishment of the hungry crew, Captain Gordon placed himself at the companion way, and would not permit a single one of them to go below.

"That's not the way to do on board ship," said he. "Are you all going below at once?"

"Why not?" asked Tom Nettle.

"Suppose we should have occasion to tack, or to take in sail in a hurry? Have we got to wait for you to finish your plate of chowder?"

"We are all as hungry as bears, Captain Gordon," added Frank Thompson. "We can't stand it any longer."

"Part of you must stand it half an hour longer. Captain Briskett has the helm, and the larboard watch will remain on deck, the starboard watch go below."

The captain's watch tumbled down the companion way, ranged themselves round the table, and went to work as though they had not eaten any thing for a month. As they are doing very well, we will return to the deck, and listen a few moments to the remarks of the mate's watch.

Paul had seated himself by the side of the

helmsman, and was asking questions in regard to
the reef, the depth of water in the harbor, and
other questions of interest only to nautical persons. The rest of the watch had gathered in a
group on the forecastle. It was unfortunate that
so many of the refractory spirits had been chosen
into the same watch; but there were Tom Nettle,
Frank Thompson, and Samuel Nason, all three of
whom had once been expelled from the club for
misconduct, and only been readmitted on their
solemn promise to mend their manners, and behave like gentlemen in future.

"I don't like it," said Tom; "and if the rest of
the fellows will back me up, I will go below and
have dinner with the crowd."

"I will back you up, for one," said Frank.

"And I, for another," added Samuel.

"But Captain Gordon gave a good reason why
some of us should remain on deck," suggested
one of the boys.

"No, he didn't. What is there to do? We
shan't have to touch a sail this hour — see if we
do," retorted Tom.

"But we might have occasion to do so, and for one, I am willing to observe the discipline of the vessel," said Charles Lawrence.

"I don't like the idea of having old Gordon domineering over us for a week," added Frank. "I don't care so much about the dinner as I do the spirit the old fellow exhibited. He placed himself before the companion way, just as though he had been the captain of a ship, and we were all common sailors."

"We will cure him of that before we have been with him many days," added Tom.

"I'll bet we will," answered Frank; "and I think the present is the best time to begin. How many of you will make a grand rush into the cabin?"

There were only four of them who were willing to take this rash step.

"Come on, then," said Tom, "I will go if there is only one fellow to back me up."

"We will follow you," added Frank. "Go ahead, Tom!"

"You had better count the cost before you go any farther," interposed Charles Lawrence. "You know we all promised to obey Captain Gordon in every thing he directed, whether on shore or on board."

"We didn't expect he was going to treat us like servants — like dogs."

"Captain Littleton wouldn't let him domineer over us in that style if he were here. Come on, boys," said Tom, as he led the way aft.

"Where are you going, boys?" demanded Captain Briskett, as the rebellious watch appeared in the standing room.

"Going below to get our dinner."

"Not yet; you must wait till the watch is relieved. You heard the captain's orders."

"We don't care for the captain's orders. We are not going to be treated like dogs."

"But it is necessary that one watch should be on deck all the time."

"Can you tell me why it was necessary to have the starboard watch go to dinner first?"

"I cannot; it is the captain's business to order, and mine to obey," replied the mate.

"It isn't our business to obey any such orders as that," said Tom. "Come, Paul, let us all go below, and have our dinner."

"I shall obey orders," replied Paul, decidedly.

"On deck, there! What's the matter?" called Captain Gordon, from the cabin.

"There is a mutiny in the larboard watch," replied the mate, with a smile.

Tom and Frank did not wait for any more explanations, and began to descend the ladder into the cabin.

"Stop, boys! what does this mean?" demanded Captain Gordon, rising from the table.

"It means that we are going to have our dinners; that is all," replied Tom, who had by this time reached the cabin floor.

"But my orders were, that the larboard watch should remain on deck."

"We don't care for that."

"You don't, eh?" And Captain Gordon was

19

evidently very much surprised, for whatever he had expected, he certainly had not anticipated a mutiny the first day out.

" Wasn't my order a reasonable one ? " he continued.

" No, sir ! It was not."

" It is necessary that one watch should be on deck while the vessel is under sail."

" That may be ; but it wasn't necessary that *your* watch should go to dinner first," replied Tom.

" Will you return to your duty, or not ? "

" No, *sir !* "

" You had better consider well what you are doing, Tom, before you go any farther. Captain Littleton placed me in command of the yacht, and expressly directed me to do every thing I have done, so far ; and especially to keep one watch on deck all the time, while we are under sail. Now, those of you who are willing to return to your duty and obey orders, as you promised Captain Littleton, go on deck again."

Not one of the four boys accepted this polite invitation.

"Then I am to settle this question with these four," added the captain.

"There's no settling about it; we are going to have our dinner; that's all," said Tom, pushing forward towards the table; but Captain Gordon placed himself before him, and prevented his farther progress.

"I have asked you to return to your duty; now I order you to do so; and I am going to be obeyed, even if there are some broken heads to bind up afterwards," replied the captain. "Briskett, let Paul take the helm and come below."

"Stand back, and let me pass," cried Tom, his face flushed with anger.

But instead of standing back, Captain Gordon seized him by the collar and threw him down. This was the signal for Frank to step in, and do battle for his friend. He was a stout fellow, and there was, for a moment, a prospect of a smart little battle; but the brawny pilot suddenly destroyed this prospect by laying both hands on the second mutineer, and dragging him on deck. Captain Gordon followed him with Tom, the two other refractory spirits not deeming it prudent to keep the promises they had made on deck only a few moments before.

Captain Gordon tied Tom's hands behind him, and Frank was presently reduced to the same ignominious condition. The other two were ordered to take their places by the side of the prisoners, and they deemed it prudent to obey.

"All hands on deck!" shouted the captain, as he took the helm from Paul. "Ready to go about!"

All the boys wondered what was to be done next; but the orders were promptly obeyed, and they took their stations as they had been instructed to do when the yacht was to go about. In a few moments the Flyaway, which had by this time passed the reef, and was standing up the harbor, was put about, and headed towards the open sea. No one ventured to ask any questions; but as soon as the mate had been restored to the helm, he fastened the prisoners to the rail, and gave the starboard watch orders to finish their dinners, and led the way to the cabin.

"He will have to pay dearly for this," growled Tom, when the captain had gone below. "My father is half owner of the Flyaway, and if he doesn't get turned off, it won't be his fault."

But Frank did not make any reply. His father did not own half the yacht, and he began to think he had "barked up the wrong tree," as he afterwards expressed it. He did not exactly know what to make of things, and couldn't understand why the yacht had been put about, and headed towards home. It was rather ominous, and he wished himself out of the scrape, or rather that he had not embarked in such a stupid enterprise.

Captain Gordon finished his dinner in silence, and as his brow looked as stormy as a thundercloud, not one of the boys in his watch cared to question him in regard to his future course.

When the starboard watch had finished their

19 *

dinner, they went on deck; and the captain ordered Dick to carry some of the chowder up for the rebellious portion of the other watch, while the mate, and those of his party who "stuck by the ship," went below.

When dinner was over, and all hands had returned to the deck, Captain Gordon announced his intention to return to Bayville at once.

"We haven't been gone a week yet," said Henry Littleton.

"Your father told me, if any serious difficulty occurred on board, to return home without delay. These fellows have chosen to disobey orders the first day out; and I think that is a serious matter."

"Do you hear that, Tom?" said Frank, in a whisper, to his fellow-prisoner.

"I don't care; the sooner he goes home the sooner will he be discharged."

"But we shall lose all our fun, any way."

"Can't help it; I won't be treated like a servant by my father's servant," replied Tom, loud enough to be heard by the captain.

"Your father can do what he thinks best when

I get home, but while I command a vessel all hands obey orders."

" Come, Tom, don't let us spoil all the fun. We will pay him off at another time. Don't let us break up the cruise," whispered Frank. " He's got us where the hair is short, and we can't help ourselves."

Tom at first refused to " back down," as he and his party elegantly expressed it; but Frank's suggestion to pay him off at another time at last prevailed with him, and he consented to join with his companions in trouble in an apology to Captain Gordon, and a promise to obey orders without grumbling in future. Frank therefore made overtures for a capitulation; but the captain at first declined to listen to them, and it was only upon the urgent request of the rest of the party that he finally consented to pardon the offenders and continue the cruise. It was only because he did not like to punish the innocent with the guilty, he declared, that he reversed his former decision; but if any further difficulty occurred, they would know what to expect.

CHAPTER XVII.

PAUL DISCOVERS THAT MISCHIEF IS BREWING.

IT was with more than the usual alacrity that the crew flew to their stations when the order was given to come about, and the Flyaway was soon retracing her course towards Gloucester. It was about sunset when this step was taken, and the yacht was some ten or twelve miles from Norman's Reef. She would have made a quick run of this distance, but the wind had all died out, and there was a perfect calm upon the sea. There was but little prospect of their getting to Gloucester that night, and they were too far out to anchor.

Before dark the captain had some misgivings as to the propriety of his course in continuing the cruise, for Tom and his companions seemed to be sulky, and he had several times observed them in close communication on the forecastle. But he

16 *

felt perfectly competent to manage them, however refractory they might prove to be; yet he feared their misconduct would destroy all the pleasure of the trip. He resolved to treat them as well as though nothing had happened, but at the same time to keep a sharp lookout upon them.

"All hands aft," called Captain Gordon; and the crew, including the mutineers, promptly obeyed the summons. "Boys," he continued, when they had all assembled in the standing room, "I propose, during this trip, at the suggestion of Captain Littleton, who would have carried out the plan if he had come with us, — I propose to instruct you a little in the practical duties of seamanship; to give you something to think about, while we are idling around the decks. You see that bell, over the windlass?"

"Ay, ay, sir."

"That's a very important thing on board a ship, for by it is regulated every thing that takes place, especially the watches. As we are likely to be out to-night, or at least a part of the night,

I intend to keep a regular watch on board, just as
they do in any well-regulated vessel. Indeed, it
is absolutely necessary to do so. We can't all
turn in and sleep while the vessel is on her course;
some of us must be on deck all the time. Therefore we had better have things done up in ship-
shape order."

"That is just what we want," said Henry — a
sentiment which was responded to by a majority
of the crew.

"Very well," continued the captain, consulting
his watch; "it wants a few minutes of eight
o'clock, at which time we will strike eight bells,
and set the watch."

"Which watch, captain?" asked Tom Nettle,
in rather surly tones.

"There is a rule about this matter, my lad, as
there is about every thing aboard ship. I shall
follow this rule," replied Captain Gordon, without
even looking at the speaker.

"What is the rule?" asked Henry, rather because he wished to turn the captain's attention

away from Tom, than because he was impatient to know the rule.

" The captain's watch, which is the second mate's in ships, takes the first, and the first officer's the second, on the outward voyage; on the homeward voyage the order is reversed. The starboard watch is the captain's; therefore it is my first watch to-night. It will be from eight to twelve; when the larboard watch will come on deck, and remain till four; then the starboard again till eight."

" That isn't fair," said Edward Freeman.

" Why not, my boy?" asked the captain, with a smile; for he readily perceived the objection the speaker was about to urge.

" The starboard watch will be on deck eight hours of the night, while the other watch will be up only four hours."

" Just so, my lad; but to-morrow night the order of the watches will be reversed. Give me your attention for a moment, and I will explain the matter. Continuing from the point where I left off, the starboard watch will be on duty from eight to twelve; the larboard, from twelve to four; when the starboard will come on deck; but —— "

"That will bring things just as they were the preceding night, and the starboard watch will be on duty eight hours, as before," interrupted Edward, thinking he had caught the captain this time.

"To avoid this difficulty, the watch from four to eight in the afternoon is divided into two, called the *dog-watches*."

"That makes it all right."

At this moment, Captain Briskett, who had gone forward for the purpose, struck the bell eight times.

"Eight bells! All the starboard watch, ahoy!" shouted Captain Gordon. "All the rest of you had better go below and turn in; while you sleep, pay attention to it, for when we call you, we shall want you."

The mate and his watch all went below; but, though they took to their berths, the excitement of the occasion was too great to permit them to sleep. There was a great deal of "skylarking" done in the cabin, as well as on deck, during the next hour, but one by one the boys below dropped asleep, and those on deck were soon tired of play, and called upon Captain Gordon to "spin a yarn." He was good-natured enough to comply with their request.

The watch on deck soon came to the conclusion that "sailoring" was not particularly funny at night, for there was a good deal of gaping, and not a little impatience for the eight bells that would relieve them for a while. At six bells there was a prospect of a little wind, and the yacht began to ripple through the water. The wind increased steadily till they had quite a lively breeze.

"All the larboard watch, ahoy!" shouted the captain down the companion-way, at eight bells.

"Ay, ay," replied Briskett.

But it was no easy task to rouse the sleepers, and even when they were awoke, some of them declared they were not going on deck again that night. They concluded, however, after the ex-

20

perience of the first day, that it would be better to fall in with the discipline of the vessel. They found the Flyaway making good progress through the water, which in some measure waked them up, and reconciled them to their situation. In two hours more, she came to anchor in Gloucester harbor, and the watch were permitted to go below. A lantern was hoisted on the forestay, and all hands were soon asleep.

Our limited space does not permit us to transfer the log of the Flyaway to our pages, and we must hasten on to more exciting events than the ordinary working of the vessel. The party spent the forenoon at Gloucester, and after dinner made sail for Portsmouth, arriving there at about nine o'clock in the evening; or rather at the mouth of the river, for they anchored off Kittery Point. On Monday morning, the Tenean, which lay upon deck, was put into the water, and the club pulled up to the city.

While they were absent, the wind veered round to the north-east, and there were some signs of a storm. It had been the intention of Captain Gordon to run over to the Isles of Shoals in the afternoon, but the weather was so inauspicious that he declined to carry out his purpose. The club spent the afternoon, therefore, rowing about the bay, in fishing, and in visiting the objects of interest on shore, including, of course, the Pepperell monument.

Unfortunately, Tuesday proved to be no better day than Monday; and in addition to the prospect of a storm, there was a dense fog outside the harbor. As Captain Gordon had been particularly cautioned to incur no needless risks, he positively refused to leave the harbor, though the boys had teased him from sunrise to do so. Even Henry and Paul were vexed at the delay. They had thoroughly exhausted Portsmouth, Kittery Point, and the Navy Yard; had visited Fort Constitution, Fort McClary, and the Lighthouse; in fact, there was not a single point of interest left to be visited.

All the forenoon the boys did not intermit their persuasions to induce the captain to proceed on the cruise; but he was as firm as a rock, and declared that, if they all went down on their knees before him, he would not "budge an inch."

After dinner, Captain Gordon, probably to escape the importunities of his crew, announced his intention to walk up to Portsmouth, and called for volunteers to accompany him. Captain Briskett, Henry, and Edward were all that were disposed to go with him, and he departed, leaving the rest of the crew to amuse themselves in the best way they could.

Hardly had they disappeared behind the hill on shore, before Paul noticed that Tom Nettle and the other mutineers on the first day out were gathered in a group around the heel of the bowsprit. They were engaged in earnest conversation, but in tones so low that he could not understand them. Presently Tom called one of the boys who were fishing over the port rail, and then another, and another, till all on board but himself had been admitted to the conference. Even John Duncan was permitted to share the confidence of the party.

Paul at once came to the conclusion that they were plotting mischief; but he could form no idea of the nature of the plot—whether it was to rob a hen-roost on shore, or capture the wooden fort that frowned upon them from the heights above. He was sorry to see John permitted to enter this conclave of mischief; but because his brother apparently acquiesced in the plan, he hoped that no serious roguery was intended.

The details of the mysterious scheme seemed to have been all arranged, for presently the boys separated into groups; but Paul heard Tom say the tide would begin to run out in half an hour. What this meant he could not possibly imagine, unless the boys intended to run away in the Tenean, and wanted the ebb tide to help them out of the river.

"John," said Paul, when the conspirators separated.

"Well, what do you want, Paul?" demanded John, in rather surly tones, as he joined his brother.

20 *

"There is mischief brewing there, and I warn you not to engage in it."

"Mischief?" queried John. "What do you mean by mischief?"

"Don't you know what mischief means?"

"Rather think I do."

"These boys are getting up some trick; don't you have any thing to do with it."

John made no reply.

"What is the game?" asked Paul.

"Can't tell."

"Can't you, indeed?"

"No, I can't."

"You know we all promised to obey Captain Gordon."

"I am not going to disobey him."

"If there is any thing wrong going on, it is your duty to tell of it."

"O, you can't pump me; so it's no use to try," replied John, walking away, and joining the principal conspirators in the forecastle.

"But what are you going to do with Paul?"

were the first words that saluted his ears, as John joined them.

"I don't know. What can we do with him?" said Tom, to whom the question of the previous speaker had been addressed.

"Of course Paul won't join us," added Frank.

"No; you might as well attempt to capture Fort Constitution as to make him join us."

"Are you sure we can't bring him over?"

"Don't say a word to him about it, or he will prevent us from going."

"He can't do that."

"He would find a way; he might jump over-board, and swim to one of these vessels and get assistance."

"But we want Paul; and if we keep him on board, he will join us after a few hours."

"You mustn't hurt him any way," interposed John; "if you are going to do any thing of that sort, I shall let the cat out of the bag."

"We won't hurt him," replied Tom.

"I'll tell you what we will do. We will get

him to go down into the cabin under some pre-
tence, and then fasten him down," said Frank.

" That will do first rate."

" But Dick is on board too; what shall we do
with him ? "

" Fasten them both down below."

Paul, from the frequent glances bestowed upon
him by the plotters, was satisfied that he was the
subject of their remarks; but this did not disturb
him, for, firm in his purpose to do right, whatever
might happen to him in consequence, he was prepared for any event which the conspirators might
bring to pass. He was sorry to find that mischief was brewing at all, and pained to see his
brother a consenting party to it.

CHAPTER XVIII.

PAUL IS MADE A PRISONER.

BEFORE the half hour which the conspirators had indicated as the favorable time for carrying out their mysterious project had elapsed, Tom Nettle and Frank Thompson went below to prepare the way for the execution of their scheme. In the cook room, which occupied the fore part of the hold of the yacht, Dick was busily engaged in scraping potatoes. This seemed to be the favorite occupation of the steward, for he spent a large share of his time between meals in this employment; and fried potatoes was the standard dish for breakfast, dinner, and supper.

"I'm glad you come down, Tom; I want to use you a few moments," said Dick, as the two boys entered the cook room.

"Well, what do you want, Dick?"

"I want you to help me move the stove; the pipe is loose; and if you will just hold it while I slide the stove back two or three inches, it will make it all right. Just hold the pipe up while I push the stove back."

"I have just cleaned up, Dick," replied Tom, who never hesitated at a white lie, and not often at a black one. "Paul is on deck, and in just the trim to do a job of that kind."

" No matter, then ; I will call him,' replied Dick; and the two boys presently returned to the deck.

"Just what we wanted," said Frank.

"Don't say a word, and Dick will call him down in a minute."

But the steward seemed to forget that he intended to make a change in the position of the stove, for he did not call Paul, as the conspirators were anxiously waiting for him to do. The tide had turned, and there was no obstacle in their way except the presence on deck of him to whom they had not dared to breathe a word of moral treason.

"Paul," said Tom, at last, when his patience was completely exhausted, "Dick wants to see you down below."

In order to make the request seem like one just made, he had lain down upon the fore hatch, which opened into the apartment where the steward was at work, thus seeming to be in communication with him.

"What does he want?" asked Paul, unconscious of the trick which was about to be played off upon him, and rather pleased than otherwise at the prospect of some employment to relieve the monotony of his situation.

"He wants you to help him move the stove."

"Never mind it now, Paul," interposed the steward from below; "any time before I make the fire to get supper will do."

"I will go now; I have nothing else to do," replied Paul, as he descended the companion ladder.

"Now is our time!" exclaimed Tom. "You look out for the fore hatch, and I will take care of the companion way."

"Ay, ay, Tom, and be quick about it."

At a signal from the chief conspirator, the slide was drawn and the fore hatchway covered up, thus making Paul and the steward prisoners below.

"What does that mean?" said Paul.

"I don't know; some mischief, I suppose," replied Dick. "They are playing off a trick upon us."

"We are prisoners, any how," continued Paul, glancing at the closed hatchway.

"All the same to me; don't mind them at all, and they will soon get sick of the fun."

"But what are they about?" added Paul, as he heard the creak of the windlass on deck. "I'm afraid they are up to some serious mischief."

"Can't help it; 'taint my fault, and I never meddle with what don't concern me. All I got to do is to cook the victuals, and take care of the cabin."

Dick was utterly indifferent in regard to the conspirators, and went on scraping his potatoes, as though nothing unusual was in progress. As long as they had not carried off his cooking stove, or separated him from the ice chest, he was perfectly contented, and undoubtedly would call all hands to supper at the proper time, precisely as though every thing was proceeding in a proper and regular manner on board the Flyaway. Dick prided himself upon minding his own business; and if the yacht had been seized by a gang of West India buccaneers, his culinary operations would have proceeded with their accustomed order and promptness.

It was not so with Paul; for the creaking of the windlass, and the activity that seemed to be manifested on deck, had already suggested to him a suspicion in regard to the purpose of the crew. He was not long left in doubt, for the sounds from above soon indicated that a portion of the conspirators were hoisting the mainsail. But he found it very difficult to accept the conclusion that these indications forced upon him. The boys on deck were certainly getting the yacht in readiness to sail; yet it seemed scarcely credible to

him that they intended to run away with her.
A scheme so bold and wicked passed his compre-
hension, and he was not prepared to believe that
even Tom and Frank had the hardihood to carry
it out. But the evidences were fast increasing;
he heard the voice of Tom Nettle, as he stood at
the helm, issuing his orders with as much assurance
as though he had been regularly placed in authority.

Presently he heard the anchor strike against
the hawse-hole, and the jib rattling up the stay.
He could no longer cherish a hope that their purpose was less criminal than he had feared. He
almost cried with sorrow and vexation when he
considered that his brother John was one of the
mutineers.

"They are running away with the yacht," said
he to his fellow-prisoner.

"That's none of my business," replied Dick,
with his accustomed stoicism. "All I got to say
is, that supper will be ready at six o'clock; because why — that's the time Captain Gordon told
me to have supper."

"But do you mean to let them run away with the yacht?"

"Don't see that I can help myself;" and the steward suspended his labors for a moment, glancing at Paul as though he had a vague suspicion that he might be in some degree responsible for his inactivity.

"I think we have a duty to perform," continued Paul.

"What can we do?"

"We must get the vessel away from them, and take her back to her anchorage."

"But we can't do that. We are prisoners here; can you break through that hatchway?"

"Then you are willing to do something?"

"Certainly I am," replied Dick. "If you can tell me what to do, I will do it."

Paul seated himself by the side of the steward, and proposed to him that, at a suitable time, they should make an effort to recover the yacht, and return her to her lawful commander. Dick consented, but he was afraid they would have no opportunity to put the plan in execution, for they could hardly overcome the eleven mutineers. Yet each pledged himself to the other to do whatever could be done; but it was agreed that they should not attempt any thing without a reasonable prospect of success.

There was a stiff breeze from the north-east, and the prisoners saw the yacht lying over upon her side, which gave some indication of the rate at which she was passing through the water. They knew how dense was the fog outside, and they had some fears that her reckless managers would run her upon the rocks, which was not a pleasant prospect to them, confined as they were in the cabin.

An hour by the clock had elapsed since the yacht got under way, and it was evident from her motion that she was laboring through a heavy sea. Paul had begun to be uneasy, for he had very little confidence in the seamanship of Tom Nettle, who, he judged, was the new master of the Flyaway, and he was in momentary expectation that she would strike upon a rock, and the cabin be filled with water.

When the yacht first got under way there had been a great deal of confusion on deck. Frank had rebelled at the authority of Tom, and claimed the right to command; but this dispute had been settled, and new causes of difficulty had appeared every moment. But now the conspirators were very quiet, and Paul perceived that they had come to realize the full peril of their position. He could hear their low and earnest tones, as they consulted together in the standing room. More than once he had heard his own name mentioned, but he could not hear enough of the conversation to determine what they intended to do with him. We will leave Paul and his fellow-prisoner below for a time, and notice the condition of things on deck.

The weather was decidedly threatening. The wind was increasing in violence, and there was a heavy sea. In short there was every indication of a regular north-easter. Tom Nettle had the

21 *

helm, but his face no longer wore the confident assurance which had given him the victory over his rival in the contest for the command, and which had strengthened the doubting hearts of his more timid followers. His eye was restless, and his movements uneasy. He was not a stupid boy — only a reckless one ; and he could not help seeing that he was leading those who had trusted in him into hardship and perils which neither party had foreseen.

The Flyaway was lying close to the wind, under jib and mainsail, and was completely enveloped in the dense fog that covered the ocean. Her bowsprit was slapping the waves, and the spray sweeping the entire length of the deck. Frank Thompson was lying out upon the bowsprit, wet to the skin, peering through the fog to give timely notice of breakers, or of any vessel which might lie in the path of the yacht. The rest of the crew were seated in the standing room, most of them engaged in watching the anxious face of Tom Nettle, whose boasted seamanship was now put to the severest test.

The Flyaway dashed on, and the faces of the rebel crew became more and more anxious every moment. Another hour elapsed, and the wind continued to freshen, and the sea to rise. Dense volumes of fog rolled by the vessel, and the mutineers were all wet to the skin. John Duncan was the only one who seemed to enjoy the scene, and it was evident at times that even he had some painful misgivings in regard to the future.

"Hard a-lee! hard a-lee!" shouted Frank, suddenly jumping down from the bowsprit, and making the most violent gestures.

Tom, startled and confused by the frantic movements of Frank, unfortunately put the helm the wrong way; and the yacht, getting the wind more a-beam, plunged deeper than ever into the huge waves.

"The other way, you confounded fool!" roared Frank, as he let go of the jib sheet.

The bewildered helmsman obeyed this order; but the movement had been so long delayed that the whole crew could hear the roar of the breakers ahead of the yacht. With the assistance of his companions Tom put the helm hard-a-lee, and the Flyaway came up into the wind.

But Frank had made a greater blunder, if possible, than the confused skipper; for when he had cast off the jib sheet, long before he should have done so, the sail had blown out as far as it could, carrying the end of the sheet with it.

My young and non-nautical readers must not suppose that a sheet is a sail; it is a rope. The jib-sheet is the rope attached to the lower part of the sail, by which it is hauled in or let out, as occasion may require. On the Flyaway this rope ran through a double block, or tackle. The sail was now slapping and banging in the fresh wind, so that Frank could not get hold of it; for the heavy block threatened to knock his brains out, as it threshed in every direction.

In consequence of this blunder, when the yacht came up into the wind, and there was no jib to help her round, she fell off, lost her headway, and drifted helplessly towards the rocks. Tom was appalled at the danger that menaced them, and gave all sorts of orders; but none of them were heeded by the panic-stricken crew.

" Draw the slide, and call up Paul," gasped the disheartened skipper; and this order was understood and instantly obeyed.

CHAPTER XIX.

PAUL TAKES COMMAND OF THE FLYAWAY.

"Help us, Paul, if you can," cried Tom, as the prisoners rushed up the ladder. "You take the helm, Dick."

"Me!" exclaimed the steward. "I don't know no more about handling a vessel than I do about making a watch. Paul must help you."

"Forgive me, Paul, for shutting you up down there, and get us out of this scrape if you can."

At this moment the keel of the Flyaway grazed upon a rock, and then bumped heavily as she sank down with the sea.

"We are lost! We shall all be drowned!" exclaimed Frank Thompson.

Paul's quick eye instantly measured the peril that menaced the Flyaway, and though she continued to thump and grind on the rocks at the bottom, he did not lose all hope of saving her. The first thing was to secure the jib sheet. Seizing the guy rope which was used to haul out the main boom, he ordered all hands forward. At the end of the line there was a large iron hook, which, with a dexterous throw, he succeeded in fastening to the block. The sail was then hauled down, and the truant sheet effectually secured.

The coast line, upon which they were in danger of being dashed to pieces, extended northeast and south-west, and the yacht was still some twenty rods distant from the breakers. Paul ordered the jib to be hauled hard up on the weather side, which caused the vessel's head to swing round with the wind; then, as the sheet was eased off, she slid over the rock, and for a moment ran down parallel with the coast, and before the wind.

When this manœuvre had been successfully accomplished, Paul ran to the helm, and giving the necessary orders, the Flyaway was soon braced sharp up, and standing away from the breakers.

"Three cheers for Paul Duncan!" shouted Tom Nettle, when he realized that they had escaped the terrible fate which a moment before had hung over them. "One!"

"Hold your tongue, Tom!" replied Paul, sharply. "Try the pump, and see whether she leaks any."

The cheers were not given in the face of this sharp rebuke, and Tom hastened to obey the order which Paul had just issued. The examination revealed the gratifying fact that the Flyaway was still sound, and made no water. She had only bumped a few times in deep water, with the action of the waves.

"You can take the helm again, Tom," said Paul, when the survey was completed. "If you wish to make me a prisoner again, I will go below."

"I do not," replied Tom.

"I am not one of your number, but I should like to ask what you intend to do?"

"We calculated to go to Portland," replied the chief of the conspiracy.

" To Portland ? "

" That is what we intended."

" That is not what you told us," said one of
the boys. " You said you would only run out a
little way, and return before Captain Gordon got
back."

" That was only to get your consent to the
plan, you spoonies," said Frank.

" You are smart sailors, I must confess," replied
Paul, with a sneer. " It was easy enough to get
out of the harbor, but not so easy to get back
again."

" We depended upon you," said Tom.

" Did you, indeed ? Do you expect me to join
in such a miserable scrape as this ? "

" We will do just what you say now."

" Will you ? You are very kind. After you
have got into a difficulty you can't get out of, you
want me to join the company. You expect me to
pilot you down to Portland — don't you ? "

" We will obey your orders, Paul ; go any
where you please," said Frank.

22

"That is a great deal easier said than done. What can I do, what can any body do, in this fog? You thought you knew every thing, Tom, better than Captain Gordon. I hope you have got enough of it."

"Captain Gordon was right," replied Tom; and this sentiment was responded to by all the mutineers.

"I'm glad you have come to your senses, even at the eleventh hour," continued Paul; who, finding the conspirators were all upon the stool of repentance, was disposed to treat them a great deal better than they deserved.

"I shall not go to Portland, or attempt to go there, for I do not consider myself competent to pilot a vessel in these waters," said he. "I shall take the Flyaway back to Portsmouth harbor as soon as I can get there."

"Wherever you say, Paul, we will go," answered Tom.

It was no easy matter to run back to the harbor they had left in the dense fog that then pre-

vailed, and Paul was sorely tried to determine
what course he should take. From his study of
the chart and the information derived from Captain Briskett, he had obtained a tolerable idea of
the coast and of the dangerous ledges and islands
in the vicinity. This knowledge, however, was of
little use to him while the fog lasted. He had no
doubt that the island upon which the mutineers
had so nearly wrecked the Flyaway was Boon
Island, or one of the Isles of Shoals. The yacht
was now headed east by north, by the compass,
and a few hours upon this course would bring
them to the coast of Maine.

"Two of you go forward, and keep a sharp
lookout ahead," said Paul. "Tom, you will take
the helm, while I go below and look on the chart."

"Ay, ay," replied Tom, reassured by the coolness and self-possession of the newly-appointed
skipper.

"I would give a good deal to be out of this
scrape," continued Paul.

"So would I," frankly added Tom. "I was a

fool to think I knew more about navigation than
Captain Gordon. What do you suppose will become of us?"

"I can't form any idea," answered Paul, as he
descended the ladder.

He found that the closet which contained the
chart was locked; but he felt that the circumstances in which he was placed fully justified him
in forcing open the door, and he lost no time in
doing so. With the chart in his hand he returned
to the deck.

After questioning Tom in regard to the course
he had sailed since leaving Kittery Point, he came
to the conclusion that the land astern of them was
one of the Isles of Shoals, for they never could
have made Boon Island without tacking. But he
could not see how, with the wind north-east, and
the yacht close-hauled, she had brought up on the
Isles of Shoals. Tom helped him solve this difficulty by declaring that he had not been very particular in keeping her close up to the wind.

Having satisfied himself on this point, the youthful skipper proceeded to decide upon his future course. If he continued to sail towards the north, he was in danger of running upon Boon Island. The night was coming on, and it promised to be a night of peril.

There were only two methods open to the young navigator. He must either attempt to make Portsmouth harbor again, or stand out to sea. In the dense fog, it would be extremely perilous for him to try to find the port from which they had sailed; and on the other hand, it seemed scarcely less perilous to go to sea with the prospect of a gale before him. It was an anxious moment for poor Paul, for he felt that the safety of the yacht and of his misguided companions were in his keeping, and before God he felt responsible for them. He tried to hold a consultation with Tom and some of the larger boys, but they were utterly incapable of giving him any advice. They were completely bewildered, and looked up to Paul as children to a father, in the midst of the dangers into which they had so recklessly and criminally plunged.

22 *

The heart of the young captain was full, as he thought of his mother and his friends at home. He felt his own weakness, his own ignorance, and stealing away from his companions, he went below, and, on his bended knee, looked to Heaven for that strength and that knowledge which Heaven alone can give in the hour of peril. He prayed for himself, for his brother, and for all his companions; but especially did he ask God to give him wisdom to guide the frail bark through the perils that environed her.

The prayer gave him resolution, and, as though his earnest supplication had been heard, he felt competent to decide between the two courses which alone were left open to him. The shore was studded with dangers; and the broad ocean, though lashed into fury by the increasing tempest, was preferable to a lee shore. The Flyaway was a stiff sea-boat, and if well-managed, would ride out any gale that would be likely to come upon them at this season of the year.

On his return to the deck, therefore, he ordered

all hands to stand by the jib sheet while he took the helm himself. His directions were so skilfully given, and so well obeyed, that the Flyaway came about as handsomely as though Captain Gordon himself had controlled the manœuvre. Her course was laid exactly east, and the compass was placed in a convenient position for use.

Dick now summoned the crew to supper. Several of them looked at Paul, but no one ventured to leave the post of duty till explicit orders had been given to that effect. Half the boys were permitted to "pipe to supper," while the other half were to remain on duty.

After the meal was disposed of, Paul gave the helm to Tom, and went forward to make his arrangement for the night. The foresail was reefed in readiness for use in case it should blow too hard for the vessel to carry the jib and mainsail; the fore hatch was carefully secured to guard against the peril of "shipping a sea;" and such other preparations were made as the occasion required.

On his return to the standing room, Paul found
that Tom could not steer by compass, and he was
obliged to take the helm himself. Among the
appointments of the Fawn, there was a compass;
and Paul, more for the purpose of familiarizing
himself with its use than from any necessity, had
often steered by it. The knowledge which the
youthful mariner had thus gained was now in-
valuable to him, and he was thankful that he had
obtained it.

A long and tedious night was before him, even
though the perils of a gale should not be added
to his present trials. The steward, at his request,
brought him up an oil-cloth coat belonging to
Captain Gordon, and thus protected from the pen-
etrating mist, he gave himself up to the long and
anxious watch before him.

Darkness came down upon them, and the Flyaway still rolled and pitched in the heavy head-
sea. The wind did not sensibly increase, and Paul
dared to hope that the gale would not break upon
them. At nine o'clock he bade half the boys go

below and turn in, assuring them they would be called at one o'clock. The order was obeyed, but not one of the boys could sleep until nearly half of their watch below had expired.

Hour after hour Paul kept his position at the helm, till the clock in the cabin indicated midnight. The watch on deck had taken turns at the lookout on the bowsprit. No event had occurred to disturb the monotony of the scene, except that they narrowly escaped being run down by a large schooner. The fog had begun to dissipate, and by one o'clock they had passed entirely out of it; but the wind had increased in violence, and at this time it blew a fresh gale.

All hands were called up, and after an hour of hard labor, the jib and mainsail were taken in, and the reefed foresail set. Now, though the wind blew a gale, the Flyaway behaved so well that Paul ventured to send the watch which had served from nine o'clock below. At four o'clock, the yacht having run ten hours to the eastward, the clouds began to disperse, the wind suddenly abated, till it became almost a calm, and there was every appearance of fair weather. At this time Paul put the Flyaway about, and laid her course due west.

CHAPTER XX.

PAUL EXERCISES A STRONG MORAL INFLUENCE.

At sunrise the sky was clear, and there was not a particle of fog to be seen in any direction; but the wind had all died out, and there was a perfect calm upon the ocean. The yacht was out of sight of land, and Paul judged that she was from eighty to a hundred miles to the eastward of the Isles of Shoals. There was not a sail to be seen, and the crew were awed by the feeling that they were alone upon the ocean. Perhaps not one of them had ever been out of sight of land before, and many of them had serious doubts whether they should ever see the shore again.

After the Flyaway had rolled and pitched for an hour in the heavy sea that still prevailed, a breeze sprang up from the south-west. The bonnet was rove on the jib, and the yacht began to dash merrily over the waves. Paul ate his breakfast, and remained on deck till nine o'clock, though he was almost exhausted by the fatigue and incessant watching of the previous night; but he had trained Tom and Frank so that they could steer by compass, and at the suggestion of the former, he went below to obtain the sleep he so much needed.

As the wind continued to blow steadily from the south-west, the yacht held her course, and the young commander was permitted to sleep till two o'clock in the afternoon, when, much refreshed, he again appeared on deck. Land was in sight over the weather bow, and the boys were in excellent spirits — or rather would have been, if the record of their misconduct could have been obliterated. Frank and Tom had recovered their wonted cheerfulness, and when they sighted the land, had begun to think of the probable consequences of the mutiny in which they had been the ringleaders. It was clear enough that Captain Gordon would immediately return home, when he recovered possession of the yacht. The cruise was, therefore, about up, if they returned to the port from which they had sailed; and strange as it may seem, Frank was actually trying to persuade his companions to run for Portland.

They had all enjoyed their sail during the day, and been pleased with the novelty of their situation. It was not pleasant for them to think of the frowns of Captain Gordon, and of being compelled to sail at once for home. A majority of them would have been in favor of continuing the cruise, if that oppressive sense of having done wrong had not operated against the scheme. But the most the adventurous leader — brave and skilful now that it was fine weather and plain sailing — could accomplish, was to induce the others to consent if Paul would agree to the plan.

"Of course he won't agree," replied Frank, pettishly. "There are enough of us to have our own way about it."

"You had your own way yesterday, and we

23

came within one of being wrecked," said one of them.

"That wasn't my fault," growled Frank.

"Whose fault was it, then?" demanded Tom.

"Yours, of course; didn't you put the helm the wrong way when I told you to put it hard-a-lee?"

"And you let go the jib sheet long before you ought to have done so. That's what made all the trouble. If it hadn't been for Paul, some of us would not have been here to talk about it now."

"You are a spunky fellow, Tom," sneered Frank.

"So are you, when there is no danger near."

"How many fellows will go to Portland?" asked Frank, desperately.

There was no response, and the conversation was here interrupted by the appearance of Paul. There were enough of them who would gladly have seen the bow of the Flyaway pointed to the north, instead of the west, but the influence of Paul was so powerful that no one but Frank would consent to take the command from him.

"What land is that?" asked Tom, as the skipper joined the group in the standing room.

"The Isles of Shoals. Keep her away a couple of points, Frank," replied Paul.

"I shall keep her as I think best," answered Frank, gruffly; for he was smarting under the disappointment he had just experienced.

"Are you going to run her on the island?" said Paul, astonished at the rude answer he had received.

"I don't know as it is any more your business than mine where I run her."

"What is the matter, Frank? What ails you? What makes you so ill-natured? I hope I haven't done any thing to give you reason for any ill feeling."

"He wants us to go to Portland," said one of the crew.

"I thought you had got enough of cruising on your own hook," added Paul, with a smile.

"I'm not going back to be snubbed by old Gordon; and the rest of the fellows wouldn't, if they had any spunk at all. Come, Tom, let's keep her away for Portland."

" I will not," replied Tom, decidedly; " at least, I will not unless Paul thinks we had better go there."

" I do not think so," interposed Paul. " You have done wrong, and all of you had better get in the right path as soon as possible."

" I am willing," said Tom.

" So am I," replied half a dozen others.

" The fact is, fellows," continued Tom, very earnestly, " I have had a lesson which will last me as long as I live. This is the meanest scrape I was ever concerned in, and when I get out of it I will try to do better. You needn't grin, Frank Thompson; I am ashamed of what I have done, and I confess that I am heartily sorry for it. I did more thinking last night than I ever did in seven years before."

" Humph !" sneered Frank.

" I don't care what you say, Frank ; if it is in my power to reform my life, I mean to do it."

Tom continued his remarks in quite an eloquent strain, declaring that, in the perils of the stormy night through which they had passed, he had thought of all the wrong he had ever done, and resolved to be a better boy. Above all things, he said he had learned the necessity of obedience; and that because he had refused to obey Captain Gordon, he had been glad to obey the orders of Paul Duncan, a boy like himself.

"That schooner is bearing down upon us," said Samuel Nason, pointing to a vessel over the weather quarter.

The stranger was evidently a fisherman, and had now approached within hail of the Flyaway. In a few moments more she had come near enough to enable the boys to distinguish the persons of those on board of her.

"Captain Littleton!" exclaimed Tom, who was the first to recognize him.

"Ease off the jib sheet!" shouted Frank, as he cast off the main sheet himself, and put the helm up, so as to carry the yacht away from the schooner.

23 *

"What are you doing?" demanded Paul.

"Do you think I am going to throw myself into the hands of Captain Littleton and old Gordon? I'll bet I ain't," replied Frank.

"What are you going to do?" asked Tom.

"Get out of his way, of course; the Flyaway can outsail that craft, and we may as well have our cruise out as be snubbed by any of 'em. Ease off that jib sheet, I say. Come, Tom, show your spunk."

"I will, but in a little different way from what you want," said Tom, seizing the helm, and attempting to restore the yacht to her former course.

"No you don't," growled Frank, dealing him a heavy blow, which Tom promptly returned; and then commenced a struggle between them for the possession of the tiller.

Frank was the largest and strongest boy on board, and for a moment the victory leaned to his side. Paul, who had seconded Tom's movement by hauling in the main sheet, now rushed to the conflict, assisted by several of the larger boys. After a severe engagement, Frank was knocked down, and held till his hands and feet were tied.

This turbulent spirit thus secured, Paul took the helm, and the yacht was brought to her course again. By this time the schooner had lowered her boat from the stern davits, and Captain Littleton and his companions were pulling towards the Flyaway.

"What does this mean?" demanded the captain, sternly, as he leaped over the rail. "Paul," he continued, as he discovered his young friend at the helm, "I am astonished to see *you* here."

The boys hung their heads with shame, and Paul preferred to let some other person vindicate him from the implied charge.

"Will you explain this, Paul?" said Captain Littleton. "If it had been my own son, I could not have been more surprised."

"Paul is innocent, sir," interposed Tom, stepping forward. Frank Thompson and myself are the guilty ones. He and I got up the scrape; we fastened Paul and Dick in the cabin, and

deceived the rest of the fellows. We kept Paul
a prisoner till we had nearly wrecked the Flyaway, and then we called him up, and he saved
the yacht and all our lives."

"That sounds like a true story, Tom, and I
am glad to find you have the manliness to acknowledge your guilt. Paul, your hand; I have
been grieving over you all day, and now I am
rejoiced to find you are still true to yourself and
the good character you have hitherto borne."

Paul gave the captain his hand, and thanked
him for the kind words he had spoken.

"What was the quarrel I witnessed just before
I came on board?" asked Captain Littleton.

"Frank Thompson wanted to run away from
you, and have the cruise out," replied Paul.
"Tom and all the rest of the party opposed him,
and finally took the helm away from him by
force."

Paul proceeded to give a more detailed account
of the events which had transpired on board of
the Flyaway since her departure from Portsmouth

harbor. Tom and the other mutineers expressed their sorrow for what they had done, and were ready to submit to such punishment as the captain thought it necessary to inflict upon them. But Paul told him how penitent they had been, that Tom had promised to reform his life, and he thought they had already been severely punished for their misconduct by the terrors of the long and anxious night they had passed through. This he proved by showing that all of them had refused to follow Frank's plan of continuing the cruise.

"But they punished you more than they punished themselves, by keeping you on deck all night," said Captain Littleton.

"It was not punishment to me, for I was innocent, and they were guilty," replied Paul.

"You are right, my boy; it is guilt that makes us cowards in the midst of peril. You plead so strongly for them, Paul, that I shall forgive all except Frank. He must be a passenger in that fishing schooner, which is bound for Boston. When

I arrived at Portsmouth this morning, I learned from Captain Gordon that the boys had run away with the yacht. I supposed, of course, you had wrecked her in the gale and the fog, and I chartered that vessel, which was on the point of sailing for Boston, to go in search of you. I thank God you are all safe."

Frank Thompson, in spite of his earnest protest, was put on board the schooner, and the Flyaway's head was turned to the north. Captains Gordon and Briskett resumed their places, and Henry Littleton spent the whole afternoon in listening to Paul's animated narrative of the cruise of the yacht to seaward.

In the course of the night the Flyaway reached Portland. But we have not space to detail the adventures of the Teneans in the harbor, or to give the particulars of the race between them and the North Star Boat Club. On the following Saturday night the Flyaway arrived at Bayville, and Mrs. Duncan once more pressed to her heart her darling boys.

CHAPTER XXI.

PAUL ADVANCES LITTLE BY LITTLE, AND THE STORY ENDS.

FOR several years Paul pursued his calling as a fisherman; and as he grew older the business became more profitable. Before he was twenty-one, the mortgage on the house was paid off; and when he was free he had saved up quite a handsome sum of money, with which he purposed to extend his operations. But when he was on the point of purchasing a schooner of sixty tons, a situation as second mate of an ocean steamer was offered to him, with the promise of certain advancement as he became qualified to fill more important positions. He concluded, after mature deliberation, to accept the offer, and the fishing business was entirely given up to John, who continued it for several years, with good success.

If my young reader's imagination is vivid enough to accomplish the feat, let us step forward nine years, which will very nearly bring our story up to the present time. It is easy to jump over a long period of years in this manner on paper, but not so easy for the mind to realize the number and the importance of the events which may transpire in this time. Though we step forward over long years of toil and care, of joy and sorrow, of severe trial and patient waiting, and behold the Paul Duncan of to-day, it will be hard to believe he is not still a boy, and the skipper of the Fawn, as we have seen him in the pages of our story.

He is no longer a boy, and we can scarcely believe that he with the bushy whiskers, and the strong, well-knit frame, is the young navigator of our tale. Yet it is he; and in order that our young friends may be properly introduced to him, we will step back a day.

Ah, you don't recognize Bayville; you don't feel at home there; for every thing is changed since the young fisherman sold his wares in its streets.

Where is the cottage of Mrs. Duncan, do you

ask? Well, about two years ago, it was pulled down to give place to the more elegant structure that occupies its site. It is a very beautiful residence; not very elaborate or very costly, it is true, but a beautiful residence for all that.

Who lives there now? Mrs. Duncan, of course; and she is still an active woman, and as affectionate a mother as can be found in the whole country. You recognize in the elderly gentleman who has just rung the front door bell our old friend Captain Littleton. He is still hale and hearty, and makes a regular call every day at the home of Mrs. Duncan. He is in a hurry to-day, and has a newspaper in his hand.

"The Marmora has arrived," he exclaims, as he enters the room where the old lady is seated.

"You don't say so!"

"Arrived this morning, and is at the wharf in New York by this time."

"I'm so glad!" replied Mrs. Duncan, pulling off her spectacles, and wiping away the moisture in her eyes. "When will they be home?"

"To-morrow morning."

And on the following morning, Captain Littleton and Mrs. Duncan were at the railroad station,
waiting the arrival of the train which was to bring
the absent ones.   They were not very 'patient, but
at last the cars appeared, and stopped at the
station.

"There they are!" cried Mrs. Duncan, as she
stepped forward and grasped the hand of the gentleman with the strong, well-knit frame and bushy
whiskers.   A beautiful lady is leaning upon his
arm, and when she sees Captain Littleton, she
throws herself into his arms, just as the young
ladies in the romances do.

But you wish to know about this lady, and we
hasten to inform you that it is Mrs. Paul Duncan, late Miss Carrie Littleton.   No doubt you expected all this when the young fisherman jumped
overboard and rescued her from a watery grave;
and it would be a great pity to disappoint you,
especially when a few dashes of the pen will
make all right with them and with the sympa-
thizing reader.

Captain Duncan and lady were escorted to the residence of Mrs. Duncan by their happy parents, and attended by sundry brothers and sisters, all intensely delighted with this pleasant reunion. I will not tell you how happy every body is at the house on the Point; but if the reader wishes to hear about the last trip of the Marmora, he must "call at the captain's office," and obtain the particulars from him. It was the quickest passage which had yet been made, and Captain Duncan was almost as proud of his ship as he was of his wife.

Little by little, Paul Duncan had worked his way up from the position in which we left him ten years before, to the command of one of the finest ocean steamers that sailed out of New York. He was exceedingly popular with the public, and was often quoted as the noblest specimen of a gallant captain, and, at the same time, a true Christian gentleman. He is not rich, as wealth is measured in our day, though he has some property, and receives a liberal salary from the Steamship Company; but in the higher and truer sense, he is rich — rich in the possession of a noble and lofty character, and a faith which reaches beyond the treasures of this world.

John Duncan still continues to follow the fishing business, and owns a fine schooner, which is engaged in mackerel catching most of the time. He is the same bold, daring fellow that we knew on board the Fawn, — which, by the way, is the name of his schooner, — and is noted for carrying sail longer than any other skipper in the fleet, thus putting the nerves of his crew to the severest trials.

Now, reader, if you like the character of Paul Duncan, build up one like it. Be true to yourself, to your parents, and to your God; be patient and persevering, and you will obtain your full measure of success, though like him you are obliged to win it LITTLE BY LITTLE.

www.ingramcontent.com/pod-product-compliance
Lightning Source LLC
Chambersburg PA
CBHW060606030726
47498CB00005B/1569